TALES
FROM THE
TORTILLA
CURTAIN
AND OTHER STORIES

ROLANDO J. DIAZ

Outskirts Press, Inc.
Denver, Colorado

JUN - - 2022

Outskirts Press
http://www.outskirtspress.com

ISBN-13: 978-1-4327-0493-3

TABLE OF CONTENTS

INTRODUCTION

Presented here is a collection of short stories and musings that have come about over the past twenty years. *Tales from the Tortilla Curtain* came about when we lived in Kansas back in the early nineties. After the fall of the Berlin Wall, I wondered if such a thing would or could ever be created along the U.S. Mexico border. Now, some seventeen years later, it seems to be happening. Not in the scale shown in these stories, but certainly with much of the same objective. Some might say that the dimensions of the wall presented here and everything that goes with it is absurd and preposterous. Yes indeed. Decidedly so. But so is the wall that is being proposed today. Only by taking the idea to the extreme can we illustrate the reality of what the Tortilla Curtain means.

A Traves Del Tiempo: Across Time is a collection of short stories that presupposes time travel is possible. Both of these collections a part of what I call *Hispanic Science Fiction.* Why does it seem that Hispanics, or minorities for that matter, don't seem to be represented in much of the science fiction literature of today? Well, here is one attempt. These stories came about after the *Back to the Future* series of movies. This time, however, we have two Latinos behind the wheel.

¡Haste el Behave o te Espanqueo! takes a more humorous look at the Hispanic experience. Here, as always, we see the constant balance between two cultures, two languages, and multiple identities.

I hope you enjoy these pages.

Rolando J. Rodríguez Díaz, M.A.
February, 2007

TALES FROM THE TORTILLA CURTAIN

PROLOGUE

In the late 1970's, the Mexican peso began its devaluation. At that point in time, the rate of exchange stood at around twelve pesos and fifty cents to one American dollar. It then dropped to twenty-five to one, then fifty to one, and so forth. By the mid-eighties, it devaluated to around three thousand to one. The devaluation of the peso continued. In the early 1990's there was a brief glimmer of hope when, under the leadership of President Salinas de Gortari, the last three zeros were dropped from the currency, thus making the rate of exchange three pesos to the American dollar, as opposed to three thousand to one. There was even talk that the future looked bright with the passage of the North American Free Trade Agreement. However, these improvements proved to be superficial, since the corruption within the Mexican government and the exploitation from the American government continued. By the year 2050, the rate of exchange, if it could even be called that, grew once more, despite the "new pesos", to seven hundred and fifty thousand pesos to one American dollar.

The decline of the Mexican currency led to a great civil war in Mexico in the year 2012. The descendants of the *peones* once again fought the landowners, those in control of what was left of Mexico. This civil war led to countless deaths for the Mexican people. The border between the United States and Mexico did not keep the hordes of people from crossing in search of a better life. The border did little to keep the effects of the Mexican Civil War from crossing into the United States. Raids carried out by radical militants resulted in a great number of American deaths. The solution was to fortify the border between the two countries.

Another factor which led to the building of the wall was the attacks on the World Trade Center on September 11, 2001. There are those who say that it was the work of the Taliban in Afghanistan and its militant factions who acted in retaliation to the American government. They also say that the American unions pressured the politicians to build the wall and thereby create more American jobs, knowing that the Great Tortilla Curtain would surely become a reality after what would later be called the worst terrorist attack on American soil.

In October of 2006, the creation of the first Family Detention Center took place in Hutto, Texas, just north of Austin. Here, entire families were detained on charges of being in the country illegally. This also happened to many individuals, who for one reason or another, were not able to prove their legal status in the country. Another facility was soon opened. Before long, there were many of these facilities across the country. Former maximum security prisons were used to house thousands of families. Although prison administrators tried to soften the environment superficially with plastic plants and a few scant things, they remained maximum security prisons. On one occasion, someone likened these prisons to a community college environment. Here, however, the "students" were not allowed to leave. Even when the media demanded tours of the facilities, what they were shown were cleverly designed facades of the real thing. The inmates were served pizza before the cameras, when only hours before they had been served meager provisions.

The terrorist attacks also served to further divide United States citizens from non-citizens, or home grown Americans from "foreigners". The "American Parentage" Bill, which dictated that the children born in the United States of illegal parents would not be granted American citizenship, was also passed into law around 2010. This law also preceded the "English Only" law that was finally passed, much to the dismay of all Spanish speakers. This led to continued distrust and animosity between family members on both sides of the border. The bloodshed along the US/Mexico border soon began and would continue for many years until the authorities in

Washington decided to erect a great wall that would stretch the entire length of the U.S./Mexico border.

In the year 2015 construction began on the great wall. It came to be nicknamed the Tortilla Curtain. It stretched from southern California, along the Arizona and New Mexico border, traced the Rio Grande from El Paso and ended at the mouth of the river around Port Isabel. The politicians bickered and the world leaders complained, but by 2030, the wall was complete. The wall stood fifty feet tall, and twenty feet wide, with guard stations set up every five miles along the wall. The modern technology of the time facilitated a quick completion.

It was here that the name *los escaleros* was first introduced, and it was here that the term would attain its full meaning. If *los escaleros*, or climbers as they were called on the American side, managed to scale the wall, they would be faced with a fifty foot drop on the other side. If they managed this they would have to either tear through or climb over a link fence which was topped with Constantino wire. After this they would have to miraculously survive the Claymore mines which stretched all along the length of the fence. And, of course, there was the five hundred yard run through the laser sighted, computer controlled laser cannons of the Data Systems Tracker. Even then, the poor souls who made it this far would have to deal with one more stretch of land mines, yet another ten foot tall link fence, and even more land mines on the other side.

TALES FROM THE TORTILLA CURTAIN

The stations along the wall were linked by the Data Systems Tracker, or Dusty as it was referred to by those who worked with it. Each station was linked by the central system, but controlled by one person. There were many cases of those who manned these stations who eventually went mad as they were haunted by the carnage of people, men, women, and children, that took place. In a bit of historical irony, many of these people were themselves Hispanic, and thus added to the deaths of many of their own.

On December 12, 2032, the rose bush was first seen in the middle of no man's land. It was a simple enough plant, with but one flower. Unbeknownst to anyone on the American side, on that very day, at that very time, the image of *La Virgen de Guadalupe* appeared on the Mexican side of the wall. The Mexicans celebrated, but most were in reverence. They knew that *la Virgen* was there for a purpose. The Mexican Americans took this as a sign that they perhaps were on the wrong side of the equation, that they perhaps were wrong.

Pilgrimages started toward the site on the wall where the image of *La Virgen* was clearly visible. The sad image looked down on the Mexican people.

The Mexican Civil War, however, continued. The situation grew worse with each passing year. The people hoped for only one thing: a new life in the great United States. Getting there was the problem. Against such insurmountable odds, the climbers attempted to cross the great wall. Despite such odds, there were those who succeeded.

Then there were those whose task was to keep them back and have to live with the consequences of their actions. The majority of the population just did their best to get along in their daily lives. Some grew up under the constant shadow of the great wall, while others did their best to cope with the constant contradiction of the environment in which they lived.

This is a collection of tales from people who lived on both sides of the Tortilla Curtain.

HUTTO HYPOCRISY

I first heard about the situation taking place in Hutto, Texas when I was at a conference in Austin. The way I heard it, entire families were being detained in what were called "Family Detention Centers." Family prisons, really. People who were in the country illegally were being detained here. This came to include anyone who was suspected of being an illegal immigrant.

How does one prove one's citizenship, or at the very least legal status, in this country? Driver's license? No. Credit cards? Not quite. Birth certificate? Perhaps. But who runs around with a birth certificate, or a passport for that matter, when traveling within the United states?

The irony is that the conference I was at had to do with civic participation and good citizenship. There I was, born in Mexico, son of immigrants, Hispanic, bilingual, learning about the various strategies for all of us to be of service to our fellow man, when less than an hour's drive north, entire families were being detained indeterminably because they could not prove their legal status.

I first noticed it was missing when I went to pay for my dinner at the hotel restaurant on the second evening of the conference. My wallet was gone. My identification was gone. Fortunately, I was able to charge the meal to my room. I left the waitress a good tip and made my way back to my quarters to see if my wallet was there. Perhaps in yesterday's trousers. Maybe in the blazer I had previously worn. By the night stand. In my conference bag. In my luggage. Under the bed. None of the above. I continued to search frantically, but it was nowhere to be found.

The front desk staff member told me no wallet had been turned in, but they would keep an eye out for it and let me know if it turned up. Surely, they said, somebody would find it and turn it in. It wasn't.

I walked around and retraced my steps of where I had been over the past twenty fours hours. The more time that passed, the more I panicked. I revisited every conference room, every lecture hall, every hallway and bathroom I had been in. Nothing.

The maitre di' pointed me out to a man in a dark suit as I walked by. The man was accompanied by an armed man who stood at over six feet tall in his military uniform.

"Are you the person who reported your wallet lost?" he asked.

"Yes," I said. "I noticed it missing this

morning."

"What is your name, sir?" he enquired.

"Mauricio Romero." I answered.

"Are you a citizen of the United States?"

"Yes, I am."

"Where were you born?"

"I was born en la Ciudad de México, D.F."

"You were not born here?"

"No, but I am a citizen of the United States. Have been since six weeks after I was born. My father is an American citizen, even though my mother is Mexican."

"Where was your father born?"

"In Eagle Pass." I answered.

"In a hospital?"

"Delivered by a midwife, I think. Does that matter?"

"Mr. Romero, you will have to come with us." He ordered.

"Will you be able to help me secure identification documents?"

"Perhaps. Please follow my . . . assistant," he said. Referring to the mountain of a man beside him.

We arrived at the Hutto Family Detention Facility in about an hour, once we got out of the traffic of north Austin. My less than friendly escorts did not say a word. From the outside, it seemed like the stereotypical images of what a prison looks like in the movies. Concrete block grey walls, twelve foot tall fence, Constantino wire all along the top.

Imagine my chagrin when I saw large groups of

children on the other side of the fence. They played and ran in makeshift playgrounds while their parents looked on. The faces of the parents, however, were not as seemingly carefree as those of the children. Their faces were serious, worried, sad. I could in an instant sense a feeling of tragedy in their eyes.

The man in the dark suit and his armed escort led me into the main administration facility. They led me into a room with a desk and a chair behind it and a chair in front of it.

I waited about two hours before anyone came in. I waited. There were seventy eight panels of ceiling tiles. There were six panels of fluorescent lights. I waited some more. There were eight three foot by twelve foot panels along each wall. I continued to wait. The clock on the wall had what I took to be a one foot radius. A white face. Black numbers. A black set of minute and hour hands. The second hands were red. I heard the constant hiss of the conditioned air being pumped through the black square vent on the ceiling. There were no windows. Time seemed to stand still. I waited.

I must have drifted off to sleep, because all of a sudden, I heard the rustle and click of the door and I was startled awake. A severe gray haired woman in a grey suit walked in. She carried a tablet with her. She sat down in the chair behind the desk, opened the tablet, and spoke.

"*Nombre*." she said in a flat tone.

"Mauricio Romero."

"*¿Donde nació usted?*"

"En la Ciudad de México, Distrito Federal."

"Fecha de nacimiento."

"Veintiuno de junio de mil novecientos ochenta."

"¿Cual es su dirección en la Ciudad de México?"

"No tengo dirección en esa ciudad. Vivo aquí en los Estados Unidos."

"¿Donde vive?"

"Vivo en Denton, Texas"

"¿Cuantos años tiene de vivir ilegalmente en los Estados Unidos?"

"Look," I said finally, "Why are you asking me all of this in Spanish? I am an American citizen. I was born an American citizen, even if I was born in Mexico City."

"Can you prove this?"

"No, I can't. Not right now. I lost my wallet while I was at a conference in Austin. I don't know if my pocket was picked or if I dropped it somewhere. The fact is that I don't have it on me."

"Can you call someone to bring you duplicate copies?"

"No. I live alone. I am not married. Don't even have a girlfriend. I don't have duplicate copies. I never thought I would need them. In fact, I don't have scanned or photocopies, either."

"You stated to the officers that picked you up that your father is an American citizen. This report states that he was born in the United States, but not in a hospital. Delivered by a midwife. Mr. Romero, it is difficult to prove your citizenship."

"I have a certificate of citizenship. I have a passport. I am an American citizen."

"Do you have any of these documents with you?"

"No, I don't. You know that."

"Mr. Romero, you will be processed on the charge of being in the country illegally."

"You must be joking!" I exploded. "I have a degree from U.T. Austin, a Masters degree from the University of North Texas. I am a University Administrator for Pete's sake. I have to be at work at the university on Monday!"

"If any of this is true, it will be verified, eventually. Until then, however, you will be detained here."

"If you just let me call someone."

"You will be appointed legal representation, but I warn you, the list is quite long of those ahead of you. The wait will be long."

"If you just let me get my certificate of citizenship and my passport, I can prove that I am here legally."

"How do you propose to get these documents?"

"If I can just get to my house. I have them there."

"You propose that we let you go, and on your honor, you will come back with these alleged documents."

"Yes. Send someone with me, I don't care. Denton is only a few hours drive from here."

"No, Mr. Romero, the reason this center was created is that people tended to disappear when we let them go. The "catch and release" scenario did not work. People disappeared when they were released on their honor. They never showed up for their court date. Now you are the one who must pay for it, in a manner of speaking."

She pressed a button to the right of the desk. In a few moments, two large, armed men entered the room. The escorted me out of the room, down to the processing center. They took my finger prints, didn't bother to cross reference with the Department of Motor Vehicles, I assume. Full frontal picture. Profile picture. Left. Right. Whatever belongings I still had on me were taken and sealed in a plastic bag. This included my watch. My graduation ring from college. A few business cards I had picked up at the conference. Somewhere included with these items went my sense of dignity and my sense of self.

An ill-fitting suit was presented to me. I was relived of my tweed blazer, my slacks, dress shoes, dress shirt, belt, dress socks, tie. I stood there in my briefs and t-shirt and looked long and hard at the orange jump suit draped over the chair. After a few moments, I put both legs into it, pulled it up over my waist, pulled my arms through the sleeves, over my shoulders, and zipped up the front. Beneath the chair, on the grey concrete floor, was a pair of white cotton socks and blue canvas shoes.

The transformation was complete. What had once been a self assured, respected, experienced university administrator, an affluent member of society in the United States of America had been reduced to a man, a thing, with no identity, a prisoner of the State of Texas.

I was led to my cell. It followed the same design as the rest of the "Family Detention Center." I came to find out later that this had once been a maximum security prison. Very little had been changed in the overall design of the facility. From where I stood, it was still very much a prison, only the inmates had changed. Where hardened criminals had once roamed – murderers, rapists, thieves – now entire families with children of all ages were housed. All of this, and one former university administrator.

My cell was light grey. The cement floor was a painted shade of darker grey. The bars were very much real, and yes, a whitish hue of grey. At one corner sat the commode. There was nothing there to cover me when the time came that I would need to use it. For a moment, I remembered all of the caged animals I had seen in my youth at the San Antonio Zoo. That was then. This was now. I was the caged animal now. Much like all of those creatures, I had no idea when I would again see the comfort of my own home.

The next day, Monday, I was led out to the playground. As I looked around I wondered what my secretary was doing at the moment. She probably thought I was running late as usual. I would probably walk in at any moment with all sorts of tales to tell of what happened at the conference.

I sat on a cement bench in the playground. This was to become a daily ritual. It was then that I saw her for the first time. She was small, slender. Her eyes betrayed a sense of hope, even as she tried to maintain a stern façade. She was ten years old. A child.

I approached her parents where they sat and introduced myself in Spanish. They looked at me with a sad smile and told me their names. They told me they had been there for over a year waiting for their case to be appealed. Their asylum had been denied the first time, so they waited to see if their appeal would be granted. In the meantime, they were prisoners of the state.

They told me the name of their little girl. Esperanza. Hope in English. They said she went by Hopey. I noticed that she sat in one of the swings are pushed herself slowly back and forth.

"No quisiéramos que ella estuviera en este lugar." the mother told me. *"Yo se que le va a hacer mucho daño mas allá."*

"Esta mendiga gente, ni porque es de aquí la dejan ir." the husband said almost to himself.

"She was born here?" I asked. "Why don't you send her to live with relatives?"

"Because we don't have no relatives here." The mother answered in her broken English. "The rest of our *familia esta en México*."

The bell sounded and we were all called back to our cells. As I walked back to mine, I saw where Hopey and her family lived. It was a cell the same size as mine. In one corner was a crib for Hopey's little sister. There were two bunk beds, where her parents slept. Hopey herself slept on a mat on the floor. The two stuffed animals on her mat seemed so out of place here.

I made it back to my cell and wondered how long it would be before my university would send out a missing persons report on me. How would they ever find me? I would surely lose my job. What would happen to my house, my things? I continued to wonder how long it would be before the legal representation appointed to me would take to get to my case. Can I get a hold of anyone who can help me? Any friend who would be able to get into my house and retrieve those damned all important documents?

My mind raced on to other things. How had we come to this as a nation? I had seen pictures of the internment camps in Auschwitz. I knew of internment camps which housed Japanese Americans and German Americans during the Second World War. I thought that was history. But, as they say, history has a tendency to repeat itself.

It had.

I heard Hopey's mother shout out for the guard. She said that her baby was having a terrible stomach ache. I wasn't sure which of her daughters she meant. Then I heard Hopey's faint cry. She was the one that was hurting. The guard finally came over and unlocked the cell door. Carrying Hopey in her arms, the mother followed the guard to the infirmary. They were gone a few hours. Finally, I saw the mother come back with Hopey still in her arms. She also carried a white bag with what I assumed to be some sort of medication.

Hopey died that night. Ruptured appendix. All her mother had been given were some antacid tablets and some Peptol Bismol. I came to find out later that this was not an isolated incident. The makeshift detention center also had a makeshift medical facility. There were many cases where serious illnesses were being handled in a most trivial manner with over the counter drugs, if any.

The next day I was roused from my slumber when a guard awoke me to tell me that I had to follow him to the administration office. When I entered, I saw one of my colleagues from the conference. He looked distraught and downright angry.

"Mauricio," my colleague said. "We wondered what happened to you. You disappeared without a trace. A staff member at the hotel told me what happened to your wallet. I quickly called your secretary who was able to get a hold of your apartment manager. He let me into your house. I searched all over and finally found your passport and certificate of citizenship under your bed."

"May I see those documents?" the gray haired

lady asked. Once she had them in her hand, she continued. "There have been many cases of forgery with these types of documents."

"I assure you," I said. "These are the real thing."

After a few tense moments, she pressed the button on her desk. A guard came in a few minutes later. "Please bring Mr. Romero's things. His documents have been verified. He is free to go." Turning to me, she said, "You will have to sign for your things, of course. Mr. Romero, you may want to consider carrying these documents with you at all times, to avoid this from happening again. The guard will escort both of you out as soon as you are ready."

She started to leave.

"Wait a minute!" I said. "I have just spent the last few days scared out of my wits, wondering if I was ever going to be able to leave this place, and that is all you have to say? No apology? Nothing?"

"Mr. Romero, you were the one in violation of the law. It is your duty as a citizen to be able to prove your legal status whenever a state or federal official asks for it. We were not in the wrong, sir. Have a good day." She left.

I stood there shocked.

A few days later, I sat at my desk in my office wondering if I had really been through all of that. For a time there, I was nameless and faceless. If I had not had a friend available to help me out, I would still be there. And then there was Hopey. She was a child who died because our system of government let her down. She should never have been in that place to begin with.

I also wondered where this type of think would lead this nation. What other injustices will this nation impose on so many people? The next decade would see the creation of the Tortilla Curtain and the atrocities that followed.

EL CORRIDO DEL MURO DE LA TORTILLA

Men with all your many sons
Always try so hard to cross
Illegally into south Texas
In search of a much better life.
When they started the construction
In the year twenty fifteen
We would send the Lord our prayers
That it would not be all so sad.
It is the grand Tortilla Curtain
Such a horribly big scar
Over an unhealing wound
That should not have gone this far.
All those blessed human beings
That all lose their blessed lives
Because of the American
Who punishes them for their sins.
This is a tragedy so sad
So many people will die
Death is the thing that waits for them
And its darkened grave.

ROLANDO J. DIAZ

The Virgen of Guadalupe
The immaculate Apparition
Looks down on us so sadly
And gives us her holy blessing.
Listen brother to this song
Of the great danger you'll find
If you cross the Rio Grande
That should not have gone this far.
It is the grand Tortilla Curtain
Such a horribly big scar
Over an unhealing wound
Your sepulcher you will find.

Hombres con todos sus hijos
Se atreven a cruzar
Sin permiso al sur de Texas
Pa' una mejor vida lograr.
Cuando empezaron construcción
En el año dos mil quince
Todos dábamos oración
Que no fuera todo tan triste
El Muro de la Tortilla
Es una cicatriz horrible
Sobre una gran herida
Que no debía ser posible
A todo el ser humano
Se le rompe la santa vida
El mendigo Americano
Lo castiga por su medida
Es una tragedia triste
Tanta gente va a morir

TALES FROM THE TORTILLA CURTAIN

Los espera allá la muerte
Y el oscuro porvenir.
La Virgen de Guadalupe
Inmaculada Aparición
Se nos queda triste viendo
Con su santa bendición.
Oiga hermano este corrido
Del gran peligro que hallará
Al cruzar el Rió Bravo
El sepulcro lo esperará.
El Muro de la Tortilla
Es una cicatriz horrible
Sobre una gran herida
Que no debía ser posible.

THE TORTILLA CURTAIN

I woke up angry this morning. Not so much about the current condition on illegal immigration, but because I keep getting lost in the arguments either for or against it. On the one hand, we need to control illegal immigration into this country. Yes, we need to control our borders. But the fact remains that we are a nation of immigrants. Only the Native Americans were here before us. Ironically, Mexicans are mostly *mestizos*, a blending of the Native American and European blood. They were also here before the United States became a country. Juan de Oñate had already set up Spanish missions by 1598, some twenty two years before the Pilgrims landed on Plymouth Rock in 1620.

But, as they say, the winners write the history books. The losers are relegated to second-class status and are made prime targets for exploitation. In this case, not only did the Mexicans lose a large portion of their northern territory in 1848 after the Battle of San Jacinto and with the Treaty of Guadalupe Hidalgo, they lost many of the very basic human rights and liberties as people who were given the choice to stay on land that went on to become the southwestern part of the United States. As the saying goes, "We didn't come to this country. This country came to us."

But, illegal immigration needs to be controlled. Politicians remind us that we cannot simply keep allowing these individuals to enter the country and take advantage of the socials services that they are not entitled to. But what is the reality here? These people do pay taxes. They pay taxes when they buy food, when they buy gas, when they buy any of the necessities of every day life. Where is all that money going? If they are able to buy a home, don't they also pay property taxes? Then why are they not able to send their kids to the local schools? Why don't they qualify for in-state tuition, if they have indeed paid their taxes? Are they not also entitled to social services like health care?

People continue to cry out for stronger borders and stronger legislation to control illegal immigration. Politicians are proposing that we erect a wall that will stretch from the western coast of California, along the underbelly of the United States and all along the Rio Grande to the southern tip of Texas. The Great Wall of America. The Tortilla Curtain.

Let us imagine for a moment that this atrocity is

even remotely possible. How would it be constructed? Well, given that Republicans in Washington have a history of awarding contracts to seemingly faultless, blameless, compassionate and considerate contractors, we can well believe that the main contract for this project would be handed to companies like A.I. Northbull or the Noren Corporation. In what would amount to a very efficient and wise use of tax dollars, these companies would set forth to placate the growing concern of illegal immigration into the country.

Talks are already on the table from representatives of A.I. Northbull that stipulate what they propose to build. By some estimates, the wall would be some fifty feet tall and twenty feet thick, with guard stations every five miles. Using the latest technology, all of these stations would be connected to central relay stations in places like San Antonio, Albuquerque, Flagstaff, and San Diego. All of these relay stations would be connected to the Department of Homeland Security in Washington.

The Noren Corporation is said to be responsible for the technology involved. One proposal states that there will be a barrier of Constantino wire on this side of the wall, followed by a quarter mile stretch of land mines followed by an eight foot tall fence topped with more Constantino wire. In addition to this, the proposal introduces what is called the Data Systems Tracker, a laser sighted weapons system that will use infrared laser sighted technology to seek out and destroy any moving objects between each of the guard stations. For safety and security reasons, any and all firings of the Data Systems Tracker will be confirmed by the guard on duty prior to execution.

According to representatives from A.I. Northbull and the Noren Corporation, all of this information will be made available to the news media of Mexico and Latin America. They want them to understand that they will be taking their lives into their own hands if they choose to enter the country illegally.

But the fact of the matter is that the people will still try to get across. They will still risk their lives to make it into the United States. They will all die trying. If the system works at its proposed capacity, there will be many deaths. Many innocents will die.

Is this too high a price to pay for securing our borders? I answer with a resounding YES!

But what is the alternative? That is a question that is difficult to answer. If the representatives from the A.I. Northbull and the Noren Corporation have an ounce of human decency, they will build their technology with some degree of compassion. Technology cannot replace human intuition. Given the influence of the almighty dollar, however, that is what will probably take place.

But there have to be safeguards. We cannot simply indiscriminately execute illegals who get caught up in no man's land. The designs submitted thus far would show no compassion. They would not distinguish from one person to another. Legal or illegal. They would simply do their job. And human lives would be lost. Many of them. Perhaps thousands of them.

One can only wonder about the people who will be working the guard stations. Those who will be at the controls when the Data Systems Tracker asks for confirmation of an execution. What will happen to them? Most of these people are the descendants of Mexicans who entered the country before the construction of the great wall. These are the people who will in effect be destroying their own past even as they wipe out their own future. Will they be able to cope? Can they sit there and take human life at will because that is what their job calls for? Will this all be justified in the name of National Security?

And what about the broken families left behind in Mexico? Will they be able to pick up the bits and pieces left when their loved ones are killed indiscriminately as they attempt to cross illegally? How will the brothers, sisters, spouses, mothers, fathers, and all other relatives and friends feel about the United States, knowing that this great nation under God, has destroyed their loved one? It will only fuel the growing hatred of this nation across Latin America and around the world.

The bill has been passed by both the House and the Senate. The appropriations Committee has allocated the funds and the Great Tortilla Curtain will be built.

May God have mercy on us all.

IN THE BEGINNING

In the early years, after the completion of the Tortilla Curtain, there were those who were made to stay behind and work the fields of the north. They had to work the slaughterhouses in Nebraska, Georgia, Iowa. They had to work in the fields of Texas, Idaho, Wisconsin. They were made to wear a yellow symbol "II" on their sleeves. II for illegal immigrant. There were those who claimed that it really stood for second class person. Women had to declare their children as illegals or be deported. At least these families had a distant chance to perhaps someday, when politics changed, be granted amnesty, and finally, perhaps, a legal right to stay in the country.

The internment camps of old were once again in use. This time it was not Japanese or German Americans who were housed there. This time, they housed whole families of illegals and even suspected illegals, not just detainees on their way to the border. They housed whole generations who had

31

at one time or another decided to come to this country without out the necessary documentation.

Children were separated from their parents. Many were sent away to live with families who were in the country legally. Washington sent in troops to seek out all those who chose to remain behind illegally. As the government soldiers marched in the execution of their orders, there were still those brave souls, Hispanic and non-Hispanic, who stood up against the oppression and risked everything to house the children of illegals.

Juan Ramirez, that was his name. At least that was the name on the documents and identification card he had bought. They had worked for a while, but now they had been nullified. Declared forgeries when one arm of government bureaucracy finally reached out to the other one. Once the link was made, everything was cross-referenced and people's lives were changed. Juan had always known he would be discovered. He awoke that morning tired from a restless sleep, with the persistent dream of finding his wife and children again. They had been separated when someone called the authorities on them and he had run. His wife was legal. His children were legal. They had all been born here. But he was still in the process of going through the paperwork to become legal. To be able to work he had bought the second set of papers for a thousand dollars. That was the only way he had been able to provide for his family. The five to seven years it took for his real papers had still not passed. It was an eternity to him. He contemplated putting the yellow II on his shirt and it made him nauseous.

He finally got up and made it to the bathroom. The face that stared back at him in the mirror seemed too strange and far removed from the one he knew was his. This one looked haggard and worn. The wrinkles from the constant exposure to the hot summer sun made his face older than it was.

He had worked in so many places. The lettuce fields of Wisconsin. The sugar beets of Idaho. The cotton fields of Texas. The slaughter houses of Nebraska. And he had nothing to show for it but a few dollars and a measly collection of tattered clothes.

What he did have was hope. Hope of one day finding his family. Hope of one day holding and kissing his wife. Hope of one day being a family again. He had heard that they were somewhere in the southwest part of the United States. Having spent the last seven years working under an assumed name at the slaughterhouse in Lexington, Nebraska, he knew that the road south would be difficult.

There was a bus company that took people down through Albuquerque and into El Paso, but that was a great risk. The Border Patrol always stopped those busses. People by the hundreds were arrested each day when it was discovered that they had either no documents or fake ones. He simply could not take the chance.

He thought about the railroad and perhaps jumping on a rail car, but that, too, was dangerous. His own cousin had attempted it and had been arrested just south of Wichita. Then he had disappeared. They never found his body. Juan simply could not take the risk, not if he expected to see his family again.

Desperation dictates drastic actions, and this was to be the case here. Juan had to take action. There was nothing for him in Nebraska. He waited by the side of the Seven Eleven across the street from the grain silo. He noticed the white station wagon as it pulled up to the station to get gas. Driving it was a lone white female. He watched as she slid has debit card through the slot in the machine and waited. Once she was through filling her car, she proceeded to walk around to the driver's side. Then he made his move. Before she could lock the doors of the car, Juan was sitting in the passenger's side.

"Please," he said in his heavy Spanish accent. "I need your help."

The young woman of about twenty-five was stunned. The shock kept her from saying a word. She just stared at him as her hands locked on the steering wheel.

"I don't mean to hurt you. Please. I just need to get to New Mexico or Arizona to find my family."

Juan looked into the store and realized that the attendant was looking back at him. The clerk new something was wrong and would soon be calling the police.

"Drive. Please" Juan ordered.

The young woman wiped the blond hair away from her face and put the station wagon in gear. They pulled away slowly.

"What do you want me to do?" she asked.

"I told you. I need your help finding my family."

"You want me to drive you to New Mexico? I can't do that. I'm on my way to Scotts Bluff. I live there. Look, I have about a hundred dollars on my debit card. We can pull into an ATM machine and I can give it all to you. Just don't hurt me."

"I am not going to hurt you in any way. I just didn't know what else to do." He could feel his emotions welling up inside of him. Anger. Bitterness. Resentment. Pain. "I don't want your money," he whispered through clenched teeth.

Back at the store, the clerk finally made up his mind to call the police. He had never been fond of them since they had arrested him for MIP in high school, but this was different. He knew that what he saw through the window did not make sense. The man was obviously not with the woman driving the station wagon. God only knew what he might be doing to her now. He called 911 and reported what he had seen to the dispatcher. He described the make and model of the station wagon as best he could. White woman, blue jeans. Blue t-shirt. Hispanic male. Black hair. Blue jeans. Gray baggy shirt. They were moving in the direction of Scotts Bluff.

"What's your name?" Juan asked.

"Lisa." she said, not making eye contact. Her knuckles turned pale as she gripped the steering wheel.

"I am Juan Ramirez. No, my real name is Juan Buentello Ramon. Ramirez is the name on my false papers."

"Juan," Lisa asked. "Why are you doing this?"

"I have to find my family," he said. "The Immigration people raided the plant yesterday. They arrested most of the people who worked there. By the grace of God I was late getting to work because I had a doctor's appointment. I knew something was wrong when I saw the white busses across the street. I have been hiding in vacant houses since. I don't know what else to do.

"I'm sorry. I can't help you." she said.

Up ahead they saw the road block. Five police cars and three green immigration vehicles. She began to slow down. As they approached the blockade, Juan opened the door and jumped out of the car. In an instant the officers and agents ran after him. They fired a few warning shots, but he kept running along the side of I 80. Juan reached into his pocket for his black wallet. Maybe he could fool them with his phony papers. With the wallet in his right hand, he stopped and turned around. He reached out to his pursuers.

"Gun!" the lead agent yelled. For a few seconds, the barrage of bullets riddled Juan's body. The impact of each one shocked him and made him stagger back until he finally fell backward coughing up his own blood.

Juan never knew that even as he died, the mail carrier delivered the notice from Immigration letting him know that a date had been set for his appointment. He would have been granted his permanent residency status. If he had only waited one more day.

REPORTS

Body Pulled From River

Matamoros – Firemen pulled the body of an Honduran man from the Rio Grande near the International Bridge Monday afternoon. The man was identified as Teofilo Rodriguez Campos, fireman Mauricio Fuentes said this morning. Campos carried an identification card from the U.S. Social Security program which did not belong to him, Fuentes said. Campos was about 25 years old. City police spotted the body in the river and called the firemen at about 2:00 p.m.

Body Found in River

Eagle Pass -- Eagle Pass firemen pulled an unidentified man from the Rio Grande on the far side of the river east of the Fort Duncan at 3:00 p.m. on Wednesday, Fire Department Joaquin Barrientos said Tuesday. The man was about 5 feet 4 inches tall and 37 years old. He was dressed in a white t-shirt, gray jacket and blue jeans, Barrientos said. He carried no money or identification. No wounds were found on the body which had been in the water for several days and had been chewed on by fish and turtles.

Another Body Found

Del Rio -- Del Rio Police are trying to identify the body of a drowned man found in the Rio Grande Saturday afternoon. Del Rio Police Department spokesman Esteban Olivares said a preliminary autopsy report indicates that it was ruled accidental drowning. The body was found at 6:00 p.m. on Saturday. The man was a Hispanic male in his late twenties with black shoulder length hair. He wore a white t-shirt with a red, white, and green emblem and "Mexico" printed on the back. He wore blue jeans, dark colored socks, and ankle-length boots, Olivares said.

Body Pulled from River

Presidio – Firemen retrieved the badly decomposed body of an unidentified man from the Rio Grande on Thursday, department spokesman Evaristo Lopez said today. City police called in the Fire Department when they spotted the body about 11:05 a.m., Lopez said. It was floating in the water. The body was clad only in white underwear, Lopez said. It was so decomposed that age, height, and weight are impossible to determine, he said. Firemen turned the body over to State Judicial Police for funeral arrangements.

Body Found In Canal along Rio Grande

El Paso – El Paso Police and Fire Department members pulled the body of 35 year old Mexican man out of the canal east of the Bridge of the Americas. He had been missing for over two weeks. Jesus Prado Santillana, of Chihuahua, was pronounced dead by Justice of the Peace Santos Alarcon at 7:54 p.m.. Santillana's death was ruled an accidental drowning. El Paso police spokesman Luis Miguel Sanchez said Santillana's daughter reported him missing on February 9. "She had been waiting for her father at Chamizal Park," he said.

Body Found Near Fort Duncan Golf Course

Eagle Pass -- Eagle Pass Firemen pulled the body of an unidentified man from the Rio Grande across from Fort Duncan Golf Course on Friday. The man was about 45 years old and clad only in tennis shoes and a dark blue shirt, Fire Department spokesman David Garcia said this afternoon. He had black hair, dark complexion, and a green tattoo that said *"La Virgen Nos Perdona."* He was about five feet 4 inches tall.

Body Found In River

Del Rio – Del Rio fire officials pulled the body of an unidentified drowning victim out of the Rio Grande Tuesday afternoon, Fire Department spokesman Ricardo Patino said this morning. The man was about 40 years old, with back hair and a dark complexion, Patino said. He wore a jean jacket, blue jeans, and brown and black boots. The body was spotted floating in the river at about 6:30 p.m.

Rio Grande Yields Body

Laredo – Firemen pulled the body of an unidentified woman from the Rio Grande near the industrial park Friday, spokesman Armando Torres said this morning. The badly decomposed body was clad in white underwear and a white brassier, Torres said. It was taken to Funeraria Rosales for burial, he said.

Body Pulled From River Near Bridge

Eagle Pass – Firemen pulled the body of an unidentified man from the Rio Grande near Eagle Pass International Bridge Monday afternoon, Fire Department spokesman Jesus Amaya said this morning. City police sighted the body at around 2:30 p.m. Amaya said. The man wore a white t-shirt, with green stripes, blue jeans, and a black belt. He was about 5 feet 8 inches tall. His age could not be determined because of the advanced state of decomposition of the body, Amaya said. Firemen turned the body over to Coahuila State Judicial Police for burial.

Man Pulled From River

Laredo – Firemen pulled the body of a man dressed in women's clothes from the Rio Grande on Saturday, Fire Department spokesman Armando

Torres said this morning. Police saw the body floating east of the International Bridge at about 6:30 p.m., Torres said. The man wore a blue shirt, black panties, a white bra, green tennis shoes, and six bracelets on his left ankle, Torres said. He had tattoos of the cross on his back, right shoulder, and a large scar on the right side of his back. State Judicial Police took the body to Funeraria Rosales.

Man Drowns in River
Eagle Pass – Late Friday night, Eagle Pass Police were trying to identify an apparent drowning victim who was pulled out of the Rio Grande earlier that day. The man's naked body was found near the International Bridge at about 6:00 p.m., said State Judicial Police agent Julian Campos. The victim appeared to be about twenty years old and was about 5 feet 6 inches tall. He had black hair and brown eyes, Campos said. There was no evidence of foul play. An autopsy was ordered and the body was transferred to the Saldivar Funeral Home.

Deputies Pull Body From River Behind Resort
Eagle Pass – Sheriff's deputies pulled the body of an unidentified Hispanic woman from the Rio Grande behind the Fort Duncan Resort on Thursday, Buentello Funeral Home director Emilio Ortega said this morning. The woman was in her late 20's or early 30's and was about 5 feet 4 inches tall, with a medium build. She had black, shoulder length hair. She wore a white t-shirt with the image

of *la Virgen de Guadalupe* on it, and black jeans. Ortega said the body will be held for identification for about 72 hours. He estimated the body had been in the water for about four days. "As high as the river in this time of year, the body could have come all the way from Del Rio or further," he said.

And the body count continued . . .

RODRIGO

Rodrigo showed up to work that day. He was part of the work crew. Those poor souls were destined, commanded, directed to clean up our side of the wall in various phases. The Data Systems Tracker was disabled to give cleanup crews just enough time, just enough safety, just enough opportunity to go in and pick up the carcasses. The remaining flesh. The remaining dark brown dried blood. The desiccated blood that remained after they had been disintegrated. Pieces of flesh. Pieces of bone. Pieces of cloth, hair, and finger nails that remained once the order as confirmed that yet another human life would be taken.

"How far will this go?" he wondered as he ate his breakfast that morning. What would he encounter that day? He ate his *migas con huevo*. The smell of the onions stung his nose. The taste of the salt bit his tongue. The eggs flavored whatever was left of his palate. The salsa danced on his lips. He was a Mexican American who was commanded, directed, driven at some level, to kill his own people. For that was the law of the land. That was what needed to take place. That was what the president of this great country had decided. Approved by the Congress. Approved by the Senate. Approved by the lawmakers. Approved by the lawyers. Approved by anyone with any inkling of legislation of lawmaking and of alleged human decency.

Rodrigo knew that the United States had developed this strategy to give hope where there was none. The families of the illegals believed, at some level, that their sons and daughters had made it. That they were living a good life somewhere in America. That they would one day see them again.

Rodrigo realized that he was part of a great deception. He was the reason the families of all those dead remained hopeful. He was the reason they still prayed to their god to keep their dear ones safe. He was an agent of so much false hope. For this he was paid his weekly salary. For this the United States government employed him and so many more like to him to do what they did, in the name of national security.

Rodrigo finished his breakfast that morning. He staggered toward the truck. It had once been a garbage truck. It had once formed massive amounts of trash into neat little bundles. Into neat little blocks. There had once been dignity in being a trash collector. But now, there was none. The truck had to crush flesh and bone and hair and blood into the self same bundles. Into the self same squares that meant nothing to our side but that meant the world to their side.

Rodrigo wondered what he would see that day. The remains of a woman. The remains of a man. The remains of another child innocently exposed to an early death. He wondered if he could survive yet another day. Earning another day's pay. Another week's salary.

He looked at his wife and he knew he loved her. He wondered how they might fare in no man's land. How they might fare against the Data System Tracker. How long it would take for them to become just another pile of flesh and bone. And nothingness.

He walked out. He stood at the doorway to the porch of his house. His wife looked at him lovingly, wondering if this man would ever show any remorse for what his life's calling had been.

She kissed him. He kissed her. He kissed his children. He wondered if they would ever take part in what the government had demanded of him.

His friend was in the truck waiting for him, driving the very truck that would take him to the great wall. He wondered if he would ever be able to forgive himself as he looked back at his wife standing at the doorway, their kids playing just inside. He could not help feeling that he had sold his soul so that his family might live.

He knew that his friend was doing the same thing to provide for his family. Here were two men, very much alike, yet very much different. At least, they would be, they could be, they should be very much different. They got to the junction of Main Street and Commercial Street in Eagle Pass and descended down the hill into no man's land. Past the point of no return. The gate opened. Their identification was confirmed. To the left they saw what once had been the international bridge of Eagle Pass, Texas. To the right they saw what once had been, some fifty years before, another bridge that had granted access to Mexican people returning to the United States.

On they drove to point A. Rodrigo was a devout Catholic. Surely this was against the will of God. He kissed the little gold cross that always hung around his neck and put it back under his uniform. He crossed himself and shoveled up the first pile of human remains. He looked down and saw the hand of what could have been his little girl. Nothing left but a hand. Stiff and dirty. Oily in its remains, he scooped it up and put it into the great bin that would compact anything and everything into one meaningless, remorseless block that would be delivered to the outskirts of Eagle Pass and buried in the dump of human history.

He and his partner got back into the truck and drove on. They came to yet another pile that the Data System Tracker had identified as less than human. Less than animal. But certainly illegal. There were several heads, legs and arms bathed in the brownish, reddish dew of the morning sun.

Rodrigo and his partner looked at each other. They put on their face masks to keep from smelling the decaying carcasses before them, and shoveled the human remains into the compactor. It didn't matter that they could have been their own relatives. It didn't matter that it could have been their own brothers and sisters. It simply didn't matter.

On they drove picking up pile after pile until it was time for them to take their lunch. They stopped by some dried up *carrizos* at a juncture supporting beams of the great wall. The truck itself was weighted heavily by its cargo. There were what amounted to about one hundred and fifty bodies, all neatly compacted into squares. They pulled up beside the great wall, with the land mines to the left and the actual wall to the right. They pulled out their *lonche paseado*, potatoes and beans, potatoes and eggs. The cheap sodas. They ate hungrily on this food that really had no taste. Things that didn't matter. They served only to fill their gut. Provide to them some sort of nutrition to carry on their day.

They continued on toward El Indio, for that was the juncture that was the end of their patrol. They came upon another pile of human flesh. Another pile of heads, arms, legs, hopes, dreams, ambitions, prayers not answered. They proceeded to scoop them up again.

Rodrigo knew that this was not something that he could continue for much longer. He knew that his little girl could easily be any one of these people whose remains he was shoveling into the compactor. He knew that his wife, his son, his child, his cousin, his grandmother could be just like any one of these people. He knew that he himself was a relative of any one of these people. They could be his brothers, cousins, aunts, uncles. But it didn't matter. He had a living to earn a check to earn. He needed to provide for his children and his wife. He would continue.

He and his partner were confronted by a squadron of Immigration Control and Enforcement (ICE) guards. They were quickly asked for their identification, which they so eagerly provided. They knew that they did not want to be confused or confronted as being illegal immigrants. They knew what it meant. They knew what it could mean. They knew. Deep down in their hearts and souls they knew.

And so on they drove, once the clearance had been granted. They drove on toward El Indio to the ruins of an old hotel. They stopped. It was now about 3:45 p.m. Their shift was coming to an end. They had what ever was left over from their lunch. The remainder of a soda. A half eaten taco or burrito. Rodrigo and his partner looked at each other sadly. Almost accusingly.

They decided to drive back toward Eagle Pass, toward the station. Their truck was about three-quarters full. As they drove, the drove past Loma Linda, past where the old casino had been. They drove in silence. They wondered if they would be able to do this, what they did for a living, what they did to survive, if they would be able to do all of this when tomorrow crept its ugly head in the morning due over the horizon. On they drove in silence as they watched each line come toward them and make is way beneath the vehicle.

Rodrigo and his partner showed up to work the next day, with their heads full of questions, remorse, and regret.

HOW MANY TIMES?

"Blowin'' In the Wind" played though the audio system connected to the central computer. The old sergeant looked though world weary eyes out across the river from his perch atop the wall. The large windows in his office were grimy and caked with the constantly blowing dust. He could not help but feel sorry for the people who only too willingly sacrificed themselves in hopes of a better life.

"How many times?" he asked himself. He sat there wondering what life means. "Where does the primal union of two cells eventually arrive? Where does the union of the sperm and the ovum eventually lead? Many would like to believe that it leads to the creation of a human being, with a soul, a purpose, a destiny. But is that inherently so? Are there laws that dictate where our lives will lead? Is there a great master plan that says one plus one will indeed equal two?"

He tasted his coffee and continued to himself, "The wind is like an idea. You can't see it, but you can feel its presence. I am but a mere mortal. I can only begin to speculate, begin to understand, begin to conjecture about what can be, what will be, and indeed what must be. Some one once said that it is difficult to see the big picture from the perspective of the piece. That is indeed the case for any human for any individual who has wondered why things have happened the way they have happened. Why destiny has dictated that things must be so. Where do we come from, I don't know. Why must things be the way they are now? We do not know. Is there a master plan? We can only wonder."

"The wind knocks off the old and wasted fruit from last year, from the year before, and leaves only the new crop. On the trees, the cactus, the mesquite bushes, on everything, really. It continues in its wrath. Much like the ideas that have been planted. They have grown. Now the Great Tortilla Curtain is here."

In the fall of 2006, politicians decided that they wanted a Tortilla Curtain. It first it sounded like it would be just a 700 mile wall. But before long, by 2015, it had grown in scope, in size, and in cruelty. The reports came in every now and then of another bunch that had been stopped. Some deterred and sent running back across the border. Others turned into the red mist of their own demise.

He pushed back his grey Stetson and took a drink of his bitter sweet, stale and lukewarm coffee.

That's all he had for breakfast anymore.

"This and humble pie," he said to himself amusedly.

The passing of the years could easily be traced across his face. At one time he had been a handsome man. With deep eyes that could see straight through to one's soul, he had always been a good judge of character. In an instant he could determine what a man was made of. Good. Bad. Apathetic, or a "lyin' son of a bitch."

He hated what he stood for. He hated what he had to do. But, he had to have the money to live. Not all that much different from the people trying to get over the great wall.

The knock at the door came almost apologetically for disturbing his peace. At first he didn't respond. After the second rapping, he answered almost furiously.

"Come in, damn it. I heard you the first time."

At the door stood one of the recent hires. A corporal from the insignia on his shoulder. A young Hispanic man, with a well pressed uniform and the look that betrayed his willingness to please his superiors.

"Name?"

"Corporal Richard Montemayor, sir," he said in a West Texas drawl.

"Montemayor? What the hell kinda name is that? Never heard of it. Do you mean, Montemayor?" he asked in a Spanish accent.

"Yes, sir. Ricardo Montemayor."

"Then why the hell didn't you say so in the first place? I want to get your name right if we're going to work together. Where are you from, Ricardo?"

"From right here in El Paso. Born and raised here. And you?"

"Can't say that it matters. Not any more."

After an awkward pause, Ricardo proceeded to make some conversation. "I notice that they never knocked down the old Asarco smoke stacks."

"No need to. Whose health is going to be endangered out there? The black dirt and the arsenic don't matter. Not anymore."

"You live over in one of the barracks of Fort Bliss?"

"No, sir. I have a family. We have a house over on the northeast side."

"Oh? Got kids?"

"Yes, sir. Three of 'em. Two girls and a boy."

"So you're a family man. Tell me, do they know what you do?"

"What do you mean?"

"They know you kill people for a living?"

"Well, sir. I don't think that what we do qualifies as killing people."

"What the hell is it then?"

"Well, we're protecting our borders. Isn't that what we were hired to do?"

"Yes, I suppose so. Tell me, Ricardo," the sergeant asked, "has your family always been in the United States?"

"Well, no. They came over from Juarez about

thirty years ago."

"Did they enter this great land of ours legally?"

"No."

"So what you're saying is that your parents weren't any different from the people trying to cross the border now."

"They weren't, but I am."

"How do you figure?"

"I am an American citizen. I was born here."

"Were your parents legal when you were born?"

"No. But the law says I am an American citizen because I was born here."

"The fourteenth Amendment. Birthright citizenship."

"Yes."

"So now that you have yours you would deny them theirs. Is that right?"

"Sir, I am not sure what you mean by all of this. I am a Border Patrol agent. I was hired to do my job. My past has nothing to do with this."

"Your past has everything to do with this! When the Data Systems Tracker asks you to confirm the execution of the people you give it the affirmative response."

"Sir, that is my job."

"Yes, yes it is. But how do you live with yourself?"

"Sir, there are processes in place for people who want to enter the country legally. If they really want to do it the right way, they can go through the proper channels."

"Ten for every thousand."

"I am not sure about the numbers, but I guess that's right."

"Son, what would you be doing right now if you weren't up here on this godforsaken perch?"

"What do you mean?"

"What kind of education do you have? What would you be doing if you could do anything else/"

"Sir, I graduated from Bowie High School and took a couple of years at the community college. I have an Associates Degree in Criminal Justice. I wanted this job."

"You ever drive out along where the old Border Highway used to be? You used to be able to look out across the fence into Mexico. See the big Mexican flag flapping in the breeze. Many times I sat there in my truck and looked at them carry on in their daily lives. They had faces then. There were human beings then," he said with a blank, far away look in his eyes. "Not so anymore. Now they're just targets to be eliminated."

"Sir, I was told that you have been here for many years, and that you used to be one of the best. You got so many honors from the Department of Homeland Security," he said as he looked at the withered, worn, and faded certificates of recognition on the sergeant's walls.

"That one there was presented to me by the President of the United States himself."

"Aren't you proud of all this?"

"You know, they say when the lunatics run the

asylum and everyone is insane, then it is the sane person who stands out. You never asked me if I had a family, Ricardo."

"Sir, we kind of got carried away with the discussion. Do you have a family?"

In that instant, the sergeant found himself arguing with his daughter. She had always been an advocate for human rights. Always speaking out against the atrocities perpetuated by the U.S. government against the Mexican people.

"Listen, Mary," said the sergeant in another time, another place, "We have rules in this country. Illegal immigration has got to be stopped. We can't afford to keep paying for these people to take advantage of us here in the U.S."

"My name is Maria. You named me. You should know."

"I don't want you taking part in any more of them protests! You understand me?"

"You know what I am protesting. You know what it means. You of all people should know that much."

"Things are getting crazy. You know what they are saying now? They want to arrest all of you. Un-American activities!"

"If this is un-American then I am un-American!"

"You can't carry on like that! Where do you think this is going to get you?"

"Does it matter? We need to raise the consciousness of this country! We are a nation of immigrants!"

"That may be where we came from, but that's not what we are now, Mary. You know your history better than I do. Hell, you majored in it up in Albuquerque. You know how . . ."

"What I want to know is how you can live with yourself. Every time you cut down another person. Every time you destroy one more life. Every time you asked that damned computer to kill somebody!"

"I don't ask it. It asks me."

The sergeant's recollection was brought to a quick end when Ricardo nudged him on the shoulder. "Sir, are you all right?" he asked.

"No, I'm not," he said as he took the last swallow of his cold coffee.

The call from the Data Systems Tracker came in as he put his cup down.

"Eliminate target?" it asked.

The sergeant clicked on the computer screen and looked at the lives he was about to destroy. He paused for what seemed an eternity while the computer waited for his reply.

"Eliminate target?" it asked again.

The sergeant looked at Ricardo with such misery in his eyes. The tears that should have been there had long ago dried up. There was a long pause before he spoke again.

"Affirmative," he whispered.

In an instant the images on the screen were gone. All that remained was the emptiness of no-man's land. He got up and stared out the window overlooking that cursed place.

"Sir, you'll have to report on why you hesitated on that call. General Order 911 stipulates that when foreigners are attempting to enter the country illegally, they must be eliminated on the basis of national security. One moment of hesitation can lead to a complete undermining of the protocols and policies currently in place."

"One moment of hesitation. One moment of hesitation!" he said as he snapped at the young hire. After a few moments, he said resignedly, "Tell them I'm tired, Corporal. Tired of this place. Tired of why we do this. Tired of this hell we live in." In that instant, he found himself once again arguing with his daughter.

"I have to do this!" she screamed.

"No you don't!" he answered. "You can't go to Juarez. Do you know how things are down there? They'll kill you the minute they know you're an American."

"They are Americans too, remember? This used to be their land, or have you forgotten?"

"Maria, you can't go."

In his faded memory, she walked out on him. He had heard that she was able to cross during one of the monthly openings of the international bridge. The Bridge of the Americas, on that side of the Chamizal Park. His wife hated him for it. After Maria left, she never spoke to him again. One Saturday morning she was gone.

The next thing he remembered was that fateful day when the call came in. He had just arrived at his post, with the usual cup of coffee in his hand. He had just put down his cup when the Data System Tracker interrupted.

"Eliminate target?" it said.

To his horror, on the screen he saw a group of people trying to make its way across no-man's land. Among them, he recognized his own flesh and blood, his own daughter. "Maria," he said as if all life was drained from his body.

There she was. Dressed in tattered and worn clothes just like the rest of them. She even wore the yellow II symbol almost as a badge of honor. She was no different. She knew this, and at some level he did also. For what seemed like an eternity, he just sat there staring at the screen.

Finally, the data Systems Tracker interrupted his trance.

"Eliminate target?"

He had held her in his arms as a baby. He had picked her up when she skinned her knee. He had taken her to the Vista Del Sol Hospital when she had her appendix removed. He had been there for her throughout her life. He loved her. She was his only daughter.

He thought about running out of the office and trying to get to her, but there was at least a mile between his post and where they were trying to cross. He would never make it in time. He also thought about using the intercom system to warn them off, but the speakers in the outer perimeter had long since been destroyed by gunfire and had never been replaced. All he could do was sit there and watch the computer monitor.

All of the vows he had taken were now tested. All that he stood for was now scrutinized. If he didn't do something the Data Systems Tracker would simply defer the confirmation request to another station. He knew they would give the confirmation order. He knew his daughter was doomed. He sat there as a lone tear ran down the crevices of his face.

"Affirmative."

And she was gone. All of them were gone in that instant.

"Sir?" Corporal Montemayor said as he again woke him from his recollection. "I am here to relieve you. Your shift is up."

"Yes, Corporal. That it is. Tell me, how long do you see yourself doing this job?"

"It's my career, sir. I hope to make my way up the ranks and eventually retire."

"You do, do you?" he asked disinterestedly as he looked out the window. "They never should have built this damned thing."

He paused as he walked out the door. "How many times?" Not really expecting an answer, he let the door close behind him.

About half an hour later, a call came in from the Data Systems Tracker. Ricardo Montemayor quickly turned to the computer monitor. On the screen he saw the sergeant. Out in no man's land.

"Eliminate target?"

The corporal just sat there. He knew only the cleanup crews were allowed out there. Even then, it took a mountain of bureaucratic clearances and could only be done once a year. He also knew that unauthorized entry into no-man's lands was deemed an act of treason. The life of a stranger hung in the balance. The corporal's whole future depended on whether he gave the confirmation order.

"Affirmative," he replied.

Just before the laser fired, he saw that the sergeant simply stood there, with his arms stretched out much like Christ upon the cross. The all too familiar whine resounded through the speakers. The sergeant was gone. Just then, a wind came up and blew away the crimson droplets that were left of what had once been a human being.

ALLENDE

It was America's finest hour. The great wall had stood for many years. Now a nation of immigrants savagely curtailed the lives of many thousands each year. The words on the Statue of Liberty – "Give me your tired, your poor, Your huddled masses yearning to breathe free, . . ."– became little more than empty rhetoric. It meant nothing. September 11, 2001 had seen to that. Now the nation of immigrants wanted nothing to do with foreigners. Not all foreigners, mind, you, just the ones who looked different. The ones who spoke a different language. The ones who valued different things. They were the ones who needed to be kept out. They were the ones who would destroy what American stood for.

They were the ones, ironically enough, who would go on to define what America was to become. The Great Wall of America, the Tortilla Curtain, became the New Colossus of the twenty-first century.

An early morning haze covered the Rio Grande at Eagle Pass. It was the year 2050, and the Tortilla Curtain had been up for about twenty years. The wall was not meant to keep people in, they said, but to keep climbers out. In the southwest Texas heat, one could see the drowned, broken bodies of the climbers who had met their fate in a futile attempt to come into the great United States of America without the proper authorization. Five, sometimes ten bodies a day made their way, side to side, along the Rio Grande toward the Gulf of Mexico. If they survived the climb over the great wall, the five hundred yard run between the wall and the safety of Commercial St. would inevitably set off the Data Systems Tracker or one of the Claymore mines.

Allende arrived at the Border Patrol Station at 7:45 am. He went by Austin Allende now, but his real name was Augustín Allende. He changed it to fit in more. He changed it to be more American. He changed it because he wanted to leave behind all things Mexican. But there were things that would not be left behind. There were things that would reach up from the past and reclaim one of their own.

He managed to graduate high school, unlike the rest of his relatives, and had some college hours. Thus, he managed to get his present position with the government of the United States, after working on the wall maintenance crew for eight years. The strong, bitter coffee wa a welcome relief to the morning drudgery. The maple syrup from the pancakes he had had for breakfast sat heavily within his system. Every now and then, he could swear that the maple syrup tasted just like the rotting corpses smelled. He shook the very idea from his head, but it persisted when he least expected.

Then the call came in. The alarm bells rang as the monitor picked up a Mexican woman with a child strapped on to her back trying to climb the wall. She hesitated and struggled, but finally made it to the top. Allende watched as she struggled down the other side and through a hole in the fence. There she stood, over the bodies of all those who had preceded her, about to attempt the five hundred yard run to the other side of the laser field. She started her run. The screen posed the question, asking for confirmation.

"Eliminate target?"

Allende knew that these people were not very unlike him. In fact, his own ancestors had crossed the Rio Grande back before the wall. *Wetbacks* they were called then. But now, these people, his people, had to climb a wall in an attempt to reach a new way of life. And the woman bared a striking resemblance to one of his cousins. His cousin, Sandra, could have been this woman's twin sister. She was the one with whom he shared many special childhood memories. All those family gatherings came rushing back. Sepia-toned images of faraway memories.

"Eliminate target?", the damned machine interrupted.

How could he confirm? The woman had a child, for Christ's sake! It looked very much like his own son. Not that much different. He saw the woman stop and adjust the child strapped on her back. She held it lovingly, surely making promises of the new life to come. If he let her go, his job would be over. His life, all of those years on the waiting list, everything, would be over. He thought of his wife. Her fair complexion. Red hair. The special love they had always known. He could not, would not, risk it.

"Eliminate target?"

"Affirmative."

He heard the all too familiar whine of the laser cannon, and a painful cry. The human being and its child were gone. At least their deaths had been quick and merciful. Sometimes the cannons missed their central target and would rip an arm or a leg off and the climber would lay there suffering, too low for the laser cannons to pick him up, but loud enough to be heard through the audio system.

The pancakes, that All-American breakfast, sat in his stomach like lead. Almost digesting him in kind. The taste of the maple syrup again reminded him of the smell of decomposing flesh, which he knew too well from working on the maintenance crew for the great wall. The Data Systems Tracker zeroed in on his image as he sat at his desk. It sought a reason, a justification, for his delayed reaction to the confirmation request.

TALES FROM THE TORTILLA CURTAIN

"Austin Allende
2729 Kathleen
Eagle Pass, Texas 78852
Date of Birth: 09-23-21
Employee number: 062787
Confirm."

"This is Allende. What do you want, Dusty?"

"You hesitated. Regulation demands explanation."

Allende sat up at night sometimes, trying to come up with stupid excuses that would satisfy the inane question of the machine. He quickly responded with one. "I spilled coffee all over myself. I was cleaning up when the call came in."

The machine paused for a moment, checking its video data.

"Negative. Records do not indicate a coffee spill. Records indicate unexplained hesitation. Explain."

"Humpty Dumpty sat on a wall. Humpty Dumpty had a great fall. All the king's horses and all the king's men couldn't put Humpty together again."

The machine stopped. A few moments later it resumed its normal operations. What the original programmers had failed to realize was that Dusty was not able to handle nonsequiturs. An illogical response would scramble its memory for a moment and then the system would correct itself. Fortunately for Allende, the machine would also dump the last hour's worth of memory.

"Good morning, Austin."

"Good morning, Dusty."

"Austin, I can't seem to remember the last hour. Has anything happened?"

"No. It's been quiet this morning. All is well."

"Do you wish to continue the discussion from yesterday?"

"No, Dusty. I don't. I brought a book with me today. I want to take time between calls and read."

"Understood."

He opened his book and stared at its pages. The words of his wife, Lavender, were still going through his mind. How could he live this way? Where were they to go where the ramifications of the great wall would not be felt? The minute he admitted to working at a border station people backed away in distrust and disgust. Even then the crackdown on illegals was growing more intense. Ah, yes, illegals, the status to which climbers were elevated if they managed to come into the country.

"Is your book interesting, Austin?"

"Yes. Yes, it is."

And this damned tracking system. It had no feelings. No remorse. No conscience. Targets, it called them. That's all they were to her.

"You seem quiet today. Is anything wrong, Austin?"

"No, everything's fine."

"Records indicate that the elimination of climbers and illegals is going well. Total climbers eliminated y.t.d: 62,547, 654. Total illegals eliminated y.t.d.: 250,463. The American way of life must persevere. American jobs must be protected. America for Americans. Truth, justice, and . . . "

"Dusty, you're interrupting my reading."

"Sorry, Austin."

"Over sixty-two million five hundred thousand lives had been lost. Why? That woman and her child sacrificed their lives. For what?", he thought, as he tightened his grip on the corner of the book.

The alarm rang out again. This time, the screen showed two different locations where climbers were attempting to cross the mine fields. Then the screen showed three more locations.

"Eliminate targets?"

Eleven more people would be dead within a matter of seconds. Eleven more people whose families would mourn for them. Eleven more people who had risked their lives for a better life in the United States. This time, however, Allende could not hesitate. One glitch in the program might be explained, but not two.

"Affirmative."

The laser cannons locked in on their targets and fired. The great tragedy was that the morning was still young. And then he heard it. Low, like the constant groan of a cello. Constant and full of pain. Had Dusty missed a target? The sound was human. In pain.

"Dusty, do you hear that?"

"Negative. What sound are you referring to?"

"That sound, like a groan. Do you detect any signs of life out there?"

"Negative. The field is clear of human life."

He scanned from camera to camera. Quickly surveying the images on the screens. Gruesome images and cadavers and decomposing flesh filled the screen from camera to camera. He noticed movement among the *esqueletos*.

"There! What is that?"

"Human remains. Nothing more."

"Is it moving?"

"Negative."

Allende heard the sound again. Constant. All consuming.

"Check your audio scanners. Surely you heard it that time."

After a few moments Dusty spoke.

"Negative. There is nothing out there."

"Fine. Fine. Let me get back to my reading."

Allende sat there trying to keep his eyes glued to the text in his hands. *Great Hispanic Leaders of the Twentieth Century*. He tried to keep every ghost story he had ever heard as a child out of his mind, but the sound remained. It came and went like the hot, southwest Texas wind. Full of life and death. He turned the page. The text meant nothing to him. It was just something to keep his mind off of the thing that he had to do to all those human beings.

He looked up at the screen. It revealed the impossible. The screen showed the grim images of two people walking calmly through the laser field.

The computer was programmed to sound the alarm at even the slightest motion. How could it possibly miss something like this?

"Dusty, do you see that?"

"See what?"

"Those two people on the screen. Surely your motion sensors have picked them up. Why haven't you sounded the alarm?"

"There is no one there. Sensors do not show any motion out in the field."

"But they are there, plain as day. Can't you see them?"

"Negative."

Allende never took his eyes off the screen. In an instant the images of the two people simply faded. Allende plopped back into his chair. Silent. He picked up his book and tried to read another paragraph. The words meant nothing. He looked up and saw three more images on the screen. These were other people. Not the same as the ones he had seen before.

"Dusty, do you see them?"

"Negative. Austin, are you all right? You seem to be slightly agitated."

"I suppose you don't see those people simply walking across the laser field."

"No, Austin, I don't."

"Run an all systems check on yourself. There may be something wrong with your motion or audio/visual sensors."

"Affirmative."

After about five minutes, Dusty came back online. "All systems working with established parameters."

"Establish a link with the computer relay station in San Antonio and ask it to perform an all systems check on you."

"Affirmative. Please stand by."

Allende continued to watch the screen for any other signs of life, but there were none. Every now and then, however, he thought he could hear that same groaning sound that he had heard before. Finally, Dusty came back on line.

"The relay computer confirms the results of the earlier test. There is nothing wrong with me. Is there something wrong with you?"

"No."

The alarm rang out. The screen revealed the shape of an old toothless man dressed in white. He carried a cross in his hands. Slowly he walked past the Claymore mines. He stopped at the center of the laser field.

"Eliminate target?"

What could this man possibly hope to gain by this action? There was nothing Allende could do but confirm, yet there was something strange in this man's eyes. They were hollow. As Allende closed in on the man's face he noticed that there was something very familiar about him.

"Dear God, . . . it's my *abuelito*."

"Eliminate target?"

What could he do now? How dearly he held the

memories when his loving grandfather held him in his arms. Those faraway, faded, yellow memories that he had long since forgotten. For a moment he could hear his voice in his mind.

"*Portate bien, mijito.*" the voice said.

How could Allende act now? If he destroyed this man he destroyed his past. If he failed to confirm, he would destroy his future.

"Confirm."

In an instant the figure he had always remembered from childhood was gone. Allende simply sank into his chair. Then he heard the moaning sound once again. This time it sounded even louder than it ever had before. This time it rang out with a certain familiarity to it. This time he could hear his grandfather's voice in among the collection of moans.

The screen became active yet again. It revealed a great number of people attempting to cross the area where the laser sighted cannon operated. Dusty, however, remained silent. Didn't the computer see all of those people? Was the computer malfunctioning?

"Dusty?" Allende said. "Are you picking anything up?"

"Negative."

The people began to ram their fists against any solid object they could hit until they created a sort of morbid rhythm that echoed throughout the border and up through the audio speakers in Allende's station.

"Don't you hear that, Dusty?"

"Hear what, Austin?"

"That drumming sound! That constant drumming sound!"

"If you are referring to the sound of your own heart, I hear it very clearly. Are you all right, Austin?"

"No, I'm not all right! Don't you see the people out there?"

"The entire field is clear for five square miles, Austin. Perhaps I should contact the supervisor and report."

"No, don't do that. I'm all right. Turn the monitors off and report whenever you pick anything up."

The monitors went dark, but the sound continued. The dreaded combination of the moaning sound and the constant beat filled every corner. Austin tried to remain calm despite the ever-rising tension in his head.

"Will you please turn off the audio system, Dusty?"

"Austin. The audio system is off. Are you all right?"

"I am fine!"

Suddenly there was a dead silence inside Austin's head. He breathed a sigh of relief and sat back into his chair. Then he heard a slight scratching at the door.

"What's that?"

"What's what, Austin?"

"Is there someone at the door?"

"There is no one at the door. See?"

The monitor came on and there Austin saw the face of his grandfather staring back at him. Calmly, serenely, beckoningly.

"Don't you see him standing there?"

"No, I don't, Austin."

"What about them. Do you see them?" he said, pointing at all of the other images on the screen.

"Negative. Let me open the door and let you see for yourself, Austin. There is no one out there."

"No!"

The lock of the door came away from its place within the frame. The door creaked open slowly.

"I wasn't my fault! I didn't mean to do it! I have to feed my family! What would you expect me to do?! *Abuelito! Tanto que te quise!* I didn't mean to kill you, *Abuelito*! Forgive me! Forgive me!!"

Sanchez, the relief operator, found Allende curled up against the corner farthest from the door. He held his crucifix firmly in both hands. His eyes were hollow as he stared into the blank wall in front of him.

"Humpty Dumpty sat on a wall. Humpty Dumpty had a great fall. All the king's horses and all the king's men couldn't put Humpty together again," said Dusty in a dreaded monotone that reeked of misdirection.

MORELOS

The streets of the *mercado* showed the aftermath of a wrecked economy and a corrupt government. That was not the place to be at that day and age. That was the place from which all those unfortunate souls tried to escape, even at the risk of their very lives. In one of the stores, a man watched the images on his flickering back-and-white-television. It was the image of the Mexican president calling out to the American president, "Mr. President!" he cried, "Tear down that wall!" That was Piedras Negras, Coahuila, Mexico in the year 2050.

Morelos, a man in his twenties, walked the streets of the barrios he had known since childhood. At one time, perhaps, Mexico was a beautiful country. The desert plains of the north. *La muraya.* The mountains of the south. Perhaps at one point in time this was a place to be proud of. But after the decline of the peso on the late 1970's, the country suffered a downward spiral until this civilization joined the ranks of the Aztecs and the Mayans.

But Morelos continued in his walk. The *jacales* that people had hastily built out of *carrizo* and straw belched the smoke of the fires within. "How can there be so much poverty on this side, when, less than ten miles away, people live in such luxury and abundance? Where is the justice?" he thought.

He walked past a child who played innocently with a piece of broken glass. The child pretended it was some great jewel which would save his family from the perdition of poverty. Morelos stood there, watching this semi-naked child carry on in its fantasy.

"*Es una jolla! Una jolla!*" the child said.

"What a tragic picture!" Morelos thought. Here was this child, with its stomach bloated from malnutrition, and there was little he could do about it. Or was there? The coyotes were always helping people cross the river. Could he join them? Would he try to climb the great wall and try to reach the golden country of America?

Morelos walked to the bank of the river and looked out across the border from where the international bridge had once been. He noticed some activity along the foot of the wall. Six people had just landed on the American shore and were preparing to ascend. They began to climb by grabbing hold on every crack and every crevice they could find.

There was one who seemed faster than the rest. The man was dressed in a blue and white stripped shirt, jeans, and the typical *norteño* boots and hat. Upward and upward he went. Finally, he managed to pull his body over the top of the wall. Morelos saw him disappear down the other side. After about ten minutes, Morelos heard what had come to be known as "*el sumbido de la luz*" and then heard the man scream in agony.

The other climbers froze in their climb. Two of them, the ones closer to the river, chose to dive into the muddy waters of the Rio Grande. The other three made their way down slowly and paddled back to the Mexican side. And there it stood. The pock-marked wall with the flag of the greatest nation in the world painted in all its faded glory.

Ten people were let into the country legally each year. Ten people for every ten thousand, perhaps ten million applications. What were the rest to do? Could he climb the wall? What if he managed to make it to the top? What then? If he happened to make it down the other side, would he set off a *morita* in his run to the city? Finally, if he happened to make it that far, what would he do? Where would he go? The peso was 750,000 to 1. He did have several million pesos, but where would they get him?

Still, he knew he had to do something. His family continued to go hungry. His meager earnings kept them on a diet of *frijoles* and *tortillas*, but little more. Was this what he had been brought into the world for?

No. Like Villa and Zapata, he knew he had to do

something for his people. There was no human justice for there to be so much poverty on one side of the wall and so much abundance on the other. His future, and the future of his family and friends, could wait no longer. He kept hearing the voice of his little girl.

"*¡No te vayas, papi!*" she cried, "*¡Quédate aquí con nosotros!*"

But he had made the decision to go and now here he was. Their fate rested in his hands. He had no choice but to try to cross the river. To climb the walls. To make it into *los estados unidos*. He noticed the place where the others had crossed and decided to cross there. He waded into the river and sank in the muddy water up to his chest. He moved quickly and as quietly as he could. Finally, he dragged himself out of the water on the other side. Here he rested and looked across at his beloved country, and was not sure what had betrayed him more – the corruption of his homeland or the impossibility of the country to which he aspired.

Above him stood the great wall. With his right hand he gripped the first of the hand holds and made his way up. He climbed. The rest that he had failed to get over the past few nights came back to haunt him now. The fact that he had not eaten very much in the past few days left him weak, but determined. Out of shear will he pulled himself over the top and lay there for a few minutes.

"That was the easy part," he said to himself, as he felt the strength return to his arms and legs.

Ahead of him lay the very thing that had kept him from getting this far. Although he had never seen any of this with his own eyes, he had heard of the atrocities that took place there on a daily basis. He knew what to expect, but nothing could have prepared him for what he saw next.

A field of human carnage. What amounted to pieces of decaying human flesh. Pools of dried blood. And the stench! He would have thrown up if he had had anything in his stomach.

He crawled until he came to a communications conduit running along the top of the wall and then down, perpendicular to the base. Here he saw his opportunity. Here he started to climb down. Using his feet to keep from sliding down too fast he descended. Finally, he stood there. On the ground. On this side of the minefield. On this side of hope. He watched and waited.

At dusk, he decided that he had waited long enough. If he waited too much longer, he would be too weak to run. He ran. Jumping across bodies. Across grotesque faces and arms reaching out for one last embrace.

Around fifty feet from the safety of Commercial Street he heard it. Like a *grito* from the mariachi songs of his youth, the Data Systems Tracker zeroed in on him. Morelos saw the fiery red of the beam. His wife, his children, would never see him again.

"Hither too shalt thou come, but no further. Job 38:11." This is what Morelos saw in the last moments of his life. This biblical passage had been written on signs all along the border by volunteers fighting for national security. Like Job he had been tested. And in the divine plan. Unlike Job, he had failed.

"*Perdónenme*," he whispered. And he was gone.

HE REMEMBERS

He remembers the way it used to be. Back before the wall. The way he used to feel. Alive. No restraints. No worries that could not be solved within a few days. He remembers that these were the days when everything was possible. The notion of one day climbing the pyramids of *Tenotchitlan* was a very real possibility.

The streets of this small town were always so calm right before daybreak. Even before the rising sun would creep over the *horizonte*, the sounds of clattering dishes would begin their symphony, accentuated by the sounds of *Tejano* music. Of course, it wasn't known as *Tejano* back then, just *norteño* music.

The way it used to be. Before friends began do die off in one way or another. Some by circumstance, some by their own hands. They are gone. In passing, a part of him is gone also.

He sits in his car at the top of the hill and looks down on all of the city. The great metroplex that was Eagle Pass and Piedras Negras was once indistinguishable, even in the daylight hours. Now the *pinche* Tortilla Curtain extends as far as the eye can see in either direction. It sits there like an unhealing wound between two countries. He sits there, looking down at the place where he grew up. Thinking. Remembering. Wishing that perhaps through some miracle, through science or *santería*, he might be able to make time run in the opposite direction. So that he could once again see the city the way he remembers it, not the way it has turned out.

Pero no. Time is unforgiving in its dedication to its cause. Always running forward. Always changing even the most permanent of things. They say that the only thing that is constant is change. *Es verdad. El tiempo nunca deja de su curso.* But in its course, it mows down everything in its path.

"Why is it," he muses, "that the only way we can really appreciate what happens to us is in retrospect?" When we are in the middle of life, we are too busy to really understand what is happening around us. Only when we have time to look back to what we have done can we understand, appreciate, the significance of our lives and accomplishments.

He pulls away from his post atop the hill and drives slowly. The street that runs through the top of the hill intersects with Quarry Street, and he turns left. There, at the foot of the hill, he stops to remember an old friend. He died on a tragic Thanksgiving night many years ago.

"A malfunction," they called it. "It could not distinguish between a Hispanic U.S. citizen and a Mexican illegal." An accident is what the official report called it.

It simply turned him into a rosy mist in a flash. In his death went a piece of the lives of many people. From his car, looking at the house of a departed friend he sorts through feelings of regret, guilt, and perhaps worst of all, longing. Longing for a forgotten moment in a lifetime of forgotten promises and dreams. Longing for a friend who was a brother. One who understood, really understood, a portion of his life like no one else ever could.

"Hijole, bato. ", he mutters to himself, "You died the way you lived. *Siempre en la busca. Nunca los dejabas en pas.*" Perhaps his friend was right in the intensity with which he lived his life. Perhaps that is the only way to live. Committed. Dedicated to your cause. Dedicated to your country. *"Pero no."*

He pulls away and drives to the center of the city--downtown. The way it used to be. The way it is now. It's like being in two different cities. In a way they are. The architecture may look similar, but it is hardly the same. The people may have the same faces and names, but their experiences have driven them all down their own paths. They say you can't go home again. How right they are. The reason is that both the home and the homeward bound are constantly changing. They two may share a portion of each other's existence for a few brief moments, but that is all there is. Nothing more.

Downtown. He remembers when Hotel Eagle was still in existence. The hotel in Eagle Pass. All the gringos stayed there when they come to town to train the locals on how to run the machinery and the other equipment. They would return to it after an evening at the sumbido —the whorehouses of Seco Mines. In its place now sits a parking lot for the Maverick County Administration Office of the Great Wall. History replaced with emptiness. Perhaps that is they way of things. Perhaps that is the way things have always been.

A flash of light. Tomorrow is gone. Yesterday is what remains. The Hotel Eagle stands in all its grandeur where it always has been. When is now? The architecture is what he remembers. The people who have long since passed away are once again in their regular routines.

"Dicen que acaban a construir una pared grande entre los Estados Unidos y México." says an old man as he walks by to his wife. The air is filled with commotion as people carry on in their daily lives. Yet the dichotomy that he remembers still exists. Whites in their place. Browns in theirs.

How is this possible? Science or *santería*. Delusion, perhaps. He leaves his car, which nobody seems to notice has arrived some twenty seven years too soon, and walks across Main Street. His clothes, always reminiscent of another epoch in his own time, seem to fit right in. People don't seem to notice the little idiosyncrasies in his attire which certainly place him in a period which has yet to unfold through the nature progression of sequences and events.

The Aztec Theater. Once the home of so many memories for so many people, sits there just as he remembered it. Some forgotten picture is displayed in the marquis. The smell of fresh popcorn, before they made it too good for people's health, emanates from the dark cavern within.

He stands in awe at the corner. Looking at people, walking, smiling, seeking the satisfaction of their needs. He attempts to communicate with one, but the old man does not listen. He tries again, but the silence is the same. He walks across the street to Eagle Drug, to see if someone there will listen to his pleas. He attempts to open the door. Locked. In trying to get the door open he notices that the handle is rusted and the inside dark, through the many years of abandonment. He turns around in the silence that fills his ears to see that the past is gone that tomorrow is once more.

His car is still where he left it. By the parking lot. The shadow of the great wall on the southern horizon. The hot summer sun bears down on him from its eternal perch. Always seeing. Never revealing. *"La cobija de los pobres."*

He walks to his car. *"El futuro y el pasado son la misma cosa, carnal."* That voice! He turns around. His friend. Long ago passed away, yet remembered almost every day.

"Oscar?" he asks in disbelief. "I was at your . . ."

"Funeral? Yes. I know. So was I. I was standing right next to you at the funeral home. I never saw you cry before, *ese*. Did I really mean that much to you?"

"*Chingao*, Osc. How can you even ask that question? All those memories from elementary and junior high school are always on my mind. You were there. You saw things the way I saw them. You understood."

"Sí, *carnal*, but you were the one chosen to go on to do great things. You are the one who was saved so many years ago in Arizona."

"Yes, the operation that almost killed me. You know about that?"

"*Como no*? You told me. Remember? Back in Graves Elementary School."

He looks around and finds himself in the school yard which has always haunted him even in the early hours of the morning.

"Graves. I remember this place."

"*Abre tu suitcase y examina los contenidos.*"

"What about this place?"

"*Dicen que los muertos no hablan, pero tu alma te dice todo.*"

A weeping child. Himself from an earlier time. Sitting there alone. The face is wrought with grief. Lonely. Fitting in and not fitting in with the other children.

"*Pídele perdón por lo que no has hecho.*"

"Why?"

"He still believes in climbing *Tenochtitlan*. He

still believes in the dreams that you can't even remember anymore. *Pédele perdón por lo que no has hecho.*"

"Forgive me, Role. You are still young enough to believe. Forgive me for my selfishness and shortsightedness."

"Díselo en Español para que te entienda."

"Perdóname."

The child looks up and smiles through its tears. He understands.

The heat from the roof of the car burns his arm as he awakens from his dream. The southwest Texas heat has left him drenched. He opens the car, turns it on, and turns on the air conditioner. He sits there. Waiting.

"Que padre se siente el fresco."

He turns around to see his friend again. Smiling almost maliciously.

"A que cabrón. What was that all about?" he asks.

"El pasado que siempre te persigue. You have to let go, Role. This is the place that saw you grow up, *pero ya no es tu* home."

"Home. Where the heart is. The guilt. The pain of blame. The weight of so many years."

"You didn't kill those people, you know. *Algo que nunca te dijeron. El pinche comandante dio la orden.*"

He looks out the window and sees the wall. As he remembered it. Like a great barrier. Inhuman. And Inhumane. The smoke from Piedras Negras gives it a sort of halo through the setting sun.

"I pushed the button. I have always believed this. That is what they have always told me."

"Quieres ver los documentos?"

"No. I want to see my house. Where I grew up. I want to see my room. I always felt that I belonged in that room and nowhere else."

He enters the house. He smells the *tortillas de harina* on the *comal. Carne con papas en el sartén.* Walking into his room he notices that he is alone. His friend is gone. The decorations that have been lost to time are all still there. Childhood mementos, childhood memories. All still here. Through the window he sees his mother watering the garden. She is still young. The flowers are all in bloom. The mesquite trees filled with their rattles. The hot summer breeze blows as the branches slowly sway.

"The house. Representative of so much more than a simple place to live. It is my past. These are my roots. They sold it when the wall came, and in doing so, began the eventual unraveling of our family. This is the place my mother dreams about."

"¿Ya no quieres ser culpable?"

"No."

"I absolve you. I absolve you of this great weight that you have carried. I absolve you."

The sting of the cold air on his face awakens him from his dream. He sits in his car. Downtown. People pass by. Some wear the yellow II symbol on their clothes. Others do not.

His eyes are filled with tears. His face is wet.

He drives up Main Street and heads out of town. As he turns left onto Highway 57, he smiles. He remembers, but he smiles. A brochure of *Tenochtitlan* looks up at him from the passenger's seat next to him.

THE GUARDIAN

Here I am. The guardian of the freedoms that we have worked so hard to protect. Yet, as I look out across the barren that is northern Mexico, I can only wonder if we are doing the right thing. So many have died, so many will die, in their daily attempt to cross the river for a better life. I look out across to see if there are any brave souls that are going to attempt this today. I wonder about the lives that they leave behind. Wonder about the dreams they are hoping for realize. Where does it all end?

They only want what any of us would want. A secure future. To be able to feed their families. To be able to educate their young. And yet, it is my job to protect our land. And our values.

But what values are these that we are trying to protect? Life, liberty, and the pursuit of happiness? Is this what we are denying them? People still maintain that so many of these people are simply coming over to take advantage of our resources. But what resources of theirs have we taken advantage of? Wasn't all of this Mexico at one point?

The Wall now protects everything. But, it only protects the southwestern part of the United States. All that once was Mexico. There is a myth that I have heard about. They say many of these individuals come across in search of the promised land of Aztlán. The land of plenty. The land of good fortune. Even now, they maintain that the streets of that mythical land are paved with gold, and that you can sweep money up with a broom.

In a way they're right. How many of us have failed to pick up a penny, nickel or dime that we see on the street? In the United States, these coins don't seem to buy much, but in Mexico, they could mean a day's ration of food, drink, or of anything imaginable. Is this what we are fighting for?

My ancestors came over as illegals back in the mid 1970's and before that. The Spanish crown deeded so much of this land to Mexicans. Of course, because of the Monroe Doctrine, or Manifest Destiny, the United States took it upon itself to decide who could and who could not live within its borders. They felt that they had the God-given right to decide who would live and who would die.

The Treaty of Guadalupe Hidalgo guaranteed basic human rights to Mexicans who chose to stay in the United States after Santa Anna forfeited so much of northern Mexico after the Battle of San Jacinto.

From where I sit I see a single rose bush that stands with only one bloom. In the midst of ashes and doom, one lonely flower defiantly holds on in the wind and rain. It sits there in its passion, in its crimson commitment, to hold on. As if the entire survival of the bush itself depends on this one bloom. It cannot, and it will not, give up.

Still here I sit, like a vulture. Feeding upon the lives and the deaths that I make happen. Wondering about the lives I spare and the lives I take away. I am that I am.

EL CORRIDO DEL SANTO DE LA PARED

They say the Saint always appears
When escaleros are in danger
When death is imminent
When immigration is on them.
When and if people ask
For a blessed hand
For death is always close behind
When they enter this great nation.
They say the Saint is simply a man
Who once worked along the wall
Who once took thousands of lives
A thing he has grown to hate.
They also say he is a witch man
With powers from the beyond.
Others say he is a traitor
With roots from over here.
The church claims the Saint
As a soldier of the Almighty

Who saves the lives
Of all of us.
People say he always
Leaves a rose when he appears
Because to the Dark Virgin
He will grant all her wishes.
I know the Saint will help me
When I find myself in the beyond.
He will hear my prayers
And forgive my sins.
They say the Saint appears
When our people are in danger
When immigration is close behind.
When death is imminent

Dicen que el santo se aparece
Cuando los escaleros están en peligro
Cuando la muerte es eminente
Cuando tienen encima la migra.
Siempre y cuando la gente le pide
Una mano de bendición
Porque la muerte siempre los sigue
Cuando entran a la gran nación.
Dicen que el Santo es simple un hombre
Que trabajaba en la pared
Quien tomo miles de vidas
Algo que llego a aborrecer
También se dice que él es un curandero
Con poderes del más allá.
Otros dicen que es traicionero
Con sus raíces de por acá.

TALES FROM THE TORTILLA CURTAIN

La iglesia dice que el Santo
Es un soldado de Dio Poderoso
Quien salva las vidas
De todos nosotros.
La gente platica que siempre
Deja una rosa cuando se aparece
Porque a la Virgen Morena
Todo los favores se los complace.
Yo se que el Santo me ayudara
Cuando me encuentre en el más allá.
Oirá mis oraciones
Y mis pecados perdonará
Dicen que el Santo se aparece
Cuando nuestra gente esta en peligro
Cuando la muerte es eminente
Cuando tienen encima la migra.

EL SANTO DE LA PARED

For every horror, there is hope. For every act of violence, there is an act of contrition. In the midst of the carnage of the Tortilla Curtain, there were still *milagros* that happened. People who made it across, despite all odds. People who experienced what they knew to be divine intervention. From one of these Santos comes this soliloquy to the soul.

"Some people say that I am a supernatural being. A Mexican *curandero*, a *brujo* with supernatural powers. Still others say that I am simply a guard who'd had enough. Simply a man who has killed enough people and who needs to atone for my crimes against humanity.

I dress all in black. They never see my face. I help people cross the mine fields of no man's land and into the United States. It's three o'clock in the morning. I've been sitting here in the moonlight. I wait somewhere between light and shadow. I wait

103

for the next group to come through. I know exactly what path they take. I know exactly what route they take. I also know exactly which perils lie before them.

I see them coming. A group of about ten people, mostly men and a few women. There's one weakness in the wall. One area that is not patrolled and that is not as sensitive to the Data System Tracker's omniscient eye. I see them about five hundred yards away. They crawl one by one. They have made it over the wall. The last one has just dropped to join the group.

I approach them quickly, in my clothes of shadows. They stand there in awe of what they perceive. They think I am a phantasm, a ghost, *un espirito*, for I will not show my face. I am there to warn them. There to guide them through the path they must take to make it past no man's land, and ultimately into the United States.

Tengan cuidado, I say *ahora están en mucho peligro. Tienen que seguirme a mi. Si no, todos morirán*. Be careful, I say. You are all in great danger. You must follow me. If you don't, you will all die. I notice that at first they are not sure about what to do. I approach the person who appears to be their leader.

En el nombre de la Virgen de Guadalupe, les pido, les aconsejo que me sigan. Síganme y yo los salvare. In the name of la Virgen de Guadalupe, I ask you, I advise you, to follow me. Follow me and I will save you. They ask me who I am. I say, *Una alma derrotada*. A broken soul. *Que anda tratando de salvar a otras almas*. One that is trying to save other souls. *Y tal vez, podrá salvar su propia alma cuando llegue su día de morir*. Perhaps, he will be able to save his own soul, when his day to die finally comes.

I lead them through no man's land, for I know when the Data Systems Tracker focuses its attention elsewhere. I've got it timed perfectly. I know how to stay in the shadows and avoid the constant eye that follows all. Of all this technology, when I am in my other life, I observe and study exactly where the land mines are, and where the weaknesses in the chain link fence are located. I've committed all that to memory.

Now as I guide these poor souls through the perils of no man's land, I ask them to step where I step. Follow my lead. I must do this.

We continue to crawl. Hoping again that my timing is correct and that the patterns haven't been changed. We finally make it through no man's land, past the final link of fence. There in the darkness I find the strong box I had hidden before. There I find documents, false though they are, and money to give these people. So that they might have a better chance of making it in this great country of ours.

The bless me. They thank me. They hug me. But they do not absolve me.

I will not show my face.

Dicen que soy un santo. They say I am a saint. I am not sure of that. But I know that I must do this.

As they walk away, I flash back to all the lives I have taken. All the confirmations I have given to the Data Systems Tracker that have resulted in so many deaths.

As they walk away into the shadows, up toward Commercial Street and beyond, I stand there wondering if I will ever be able to appease my soul, appease my God for what I have done to so many.

I make my way back to my perch and sit there. Waiting for the next group to come through.

I must do this. I am what I must be."

They say that a group of saints eventually grew out of that one experience of that one man. People did not know if they were ghosts or if they were angry protesters, or simply guards who had had enough.

Sightings of the *Santos* began to be reported by many guards along the wall, and by the people who made it through. They somehow communicated back to their families in Mexico. Sightings ranged from Matamoros and Brownsville to both of the Laredos to Piedras Negras and Eagle Pass to Ojinaga and Presidio to El Paso and Juarez and all rest of the border states of the southwest.

There were too many sightings for him to be human, they said. They knew it must be a ghost. It had to be. Finally, an answer to so many prayers. Always dressed in black. No one ever saw the face. Always, the *Santo* helped, the *Santo* guided, the *Santo* protected. It came to be known *as el Santo de la Pared*. They knew that he would protect them, and they prayed to *la Virgen de Guadalupe* that he would guide them.

The reality that these were also the descendants of the militias that had formed so many years earlier. They felt obligated of their own free will and accord to protect the very people that their ancestors had persecuted. They wore the letter M somewhere on their clothing and that is how they identified themselves. A certain sign, a certain word was also used to identify themselves to each other, for they knew that if they were ever to be found out, they would surely die, for this was an act of high treason in the United States. The M became a symbol for these people. Men and women. Some were guards along the wall. Some had worked there in some capacity. They were all people who knew how to get around the technology. All of them were committed to the poor souls who would otherwise meet horrific deaths. They knew they had to do what they had to do to atone for the sins of the fathers, who were the ones who had served in militias so many years before. The ones who had proudly built fences. The ones who had proudly taken direct aim and fired on innocent souls who were only trying to get to a better life.

The *Santos de la Pared* saved hundreds, if not thousands of people. Unfortunately, they could not save them all. The human carnage still continued. They tried, for everyone's sake, for the sake of those trying to cross, they tried.

This is the experience that had to be told. The secret society of the M, otherwise known as *el Santo de la Pared.*

WHEN WE SPOKE
ENGLISH ONLY

The politicians had always threatened us with it. After the building of the Great Wall of America, or the Tortilla Curtain, as those of us who lived along the border called it, English Only became the official language of the United States.

From the get-go there were problems with the idea. What all of them politicians never took under consideration was that we was a nation of immigrants. That English, as it had evolved in this country, was an amalgamation, a uniting, if you will, of a great many other languages. There was no one language that could be given just due credit for how we talked in these here United States.

First, someone pointed out to the lawyers that many of them legal phrases were in Latin, not English. "*Quid pro quo, e pluribus unum*, and *en flagrante delecto*" were all Latin. All them laws and legal mumbo jumbo had to be changed. The "status quo" if you will, could not be allowed if'n we were to speak English only.

Then someone pointed out that we was going to have to change the names of quite a few states. The Great State of Texas had to change its name to the Great State of Friendly. Named after the friendly Indians, don't you know. Gosh, even the name of one of the largest cities in the state had to be changed. San Antonio, Texas became Saint Anthony, Friendly. Didn't do too much to inspire awe in the other states any more.

Other states didn't fare that much better. Arizona became Arid Zone, Montana became Mountain. Heck even the eastern states were affected. The state of Connecticut had to change its name, too. Cain't quite recall what they eventually went with. Course, Colorado became the Red state. New Mexico, Nevada, California, Louisiana, Utah, Florida, Alaska, the Dakotas, and many more changed their names. Had to. English Only was the law of the land.

They passed laws that stipulated that no one could speak any language other than English. Anywhere. Anytime. Work. School Home. Didn't matter. English only meant English only. Nothin' else.

Folks even started changing their names to be more American. Roberto became Robert. Maria became Mary. Everybody, no matter what language, translated their name into English. Didn't matter. They wanted to be American. Be sure they weren't mistaken for any of them foreigners. They sure as hell didn't want people to think they had to wear that damned yellow II sign on their shirts.

They changed what we ate, too. Wasn't a tortilla anymore. It was flatbread. Not a burrito, but a wrap. Heck, even beef jerky had to be changed to dehydrated meat product. Jerky, you see, was coined by the *yaqui* Indians.

Even our home décor was impacted. You know that thing over your dining table? Wasn't a chandelier anymore. French. It became crystal lighting fixture. Ahhh, the beauty of English Only.

They even changed our currency. By that time hard currency was hardly used anymore anyway, but they technically changed the name of the dollar, Roman in origin, you know, to "credit." In other words, you got so many credits an hour. Something was worth so many credits, and such.

Someone in Washington finally drew the line when someone pointed out that the great United States of America was named after an Italian.

THE DAY THEY STOPPED COMING

At first no one noticed. A penny increase here for a pound of fruit. A nickel there per pound for the price of vegetables. Maybe no one cared. We were, after all, the greatest country in the world. With the greatest economy. People made their money and bought goods and services produced by people here illegally. Part of the great economy of this country. Even the law makers turned a blind eye, as long as the crops were picked and the houses built and cleaned for a fraction of what it would cost if Americans did the work.

One day, they stopped coming. The people who built the Tortilla Curtain had at last met with the success that had long eluded them. There were no more Mexicans. None. The Great Wall, like a great dyke, finally held and stopped the waves of humanity from crashing through the border.

Then the economy started to spiral. Agricultural producers could not sell what had not been picked. Whole crops, including cotton and corn, lay rotting in the fields. No American in his or her right mind would work for below minimum wage, in hazardous conditions, exposed to pesticides and other health risks, with no insurance and no hope for career or educational opportunities. Nobody wanted to do the work that the Mexicans had done.

THE TRUTH

"(20) However, the prophet who presumes to speak in my name a word that I have not commanded him to speak, or who speaks in the name of other gods, that prophet must die. (21) And in case you should say in your heart: 'How shall we know the word that Jehovah has not spoken?' (22) When the prophet speaks in the name of Jehovah and the words does not occur or come true, that is the word Jehovah did not speak. With presumptuousness the prophet spoke it. You must not be frightened at him."

(Deuteronomy, Ch. 18, verses 20 – 22)

The truth had always bothered him. Not his truth. Their truth. It was their interpretation of the truth he had always been taught. They were the ones who had predicted that this system of things would come to an end in 2032. But who really listened to these warnings? Who really believed the words put out by the Society?

Ruben was a thin boy of average height. Now in the middle of the fourth grade, his thoughts continuously focused on the coming year. If it was all true, there would soon be an incredible change in the world. Would he be one of the chosen ones? Who would survive? What would it feel like when the world is being destroyed and you are still left there standing, unharmed?

Harlingen, Texas at the end of December of 2031 was a warm and inviting place. Sure, there had been a few cold nights, but the valley of Texas was haven to many people who chose to avoid the frozen winters of the north. People were still getting used to the idea of the Tortilla Curtain.

Ruben had read and re-read the little blue book, or *el librito azul*, as his mother always called it. It prophesied to tell the truth. The truth of things past. The truth of modern society. The truth of things to come.

All of this information really frightened Ruben. Especially now. Tonight. This was New Year's Eve. The year 2032 would arrive in a few hours and then what? The end of this system of things? For years the congregation had foretold of the coming of the end. According to them, it had all been set into motion in 1914. That was when Christ first assumed command over all the earth. This is when it all started, according to them.

Uncle Esteban, or Tio Chito as he was known to the family, was an elder in the church. His father, Abuelito Chito, had first been introduced to the religion in the late 30's, so now all of the family followed its teachings. Of course, 'buelito Chito had had two separate families, one in Eagle Pass, where Ruben's dad came from, and the other in Piedras Negras, people that Ruben would always hear about but never meet. In spite of his enlightenment with the alleged truth, 'buelito Chito would keep both families ignorant of one another for many years.

Ruben looked at the clock. 8:30 p.m. In three and a half more hours the end would come. His mother and father talked in the kitchen. His only brother watched television in the living room. Ruben sat in the darkness of his room. Waiting. Waiting like a condemned man waiting for the inevitable.

And Ruben had listened in on many conversations at church. Every Tuesday, Thursday, and Sunday, his father, Reynaldo Ruiz, had taken the whole family to church. One hour on Tuesday to study *el librito azul*. One hour on Thursday to study the *Bible*. Two hours on Sunday, to study the two magazines that spoke about modern times, and to listen to the sermons about the truth and about how God's chosen people should avoid the ways of the world.

Even as a boy, Ruben had been bothered by these sermons. Bothered by the inconsistency and downright hypocrisy of what they preached at church. Righteous people could not accept blood, they said. Even if it meant death. But wasn't life

God's greatest gift? And if a person had it within their grasp to save themselves and chose not to, was this not something like suicide? And wasn't that against God's word?

They also could not celebrate any holiday, except Passover, when they passed the wine and unleavened bread from one person to another but would never part take in any of it. Passover but no communion. How could this be? Did not the *Bible* say that we needed to eat the bread and drink the wine? Why did only the church's selected few get to do this? Was heaven not for everybody?

Tio Chito had even told many parents in the congregation that it was God's will that their sons and daughters get a minimal education. It would not be necessary in the new system of things. And many people listened and heeded his words. Many young men and women were kept from furthering their education because it was God's word, according to Tio Chito. Many years later, Ruben was really bothered by the fact that Tio Chito let his first born son, Estebanito, go to college on a four-year scholarship in Electrical Engineering. Evidently, the bright light of the truth had grown brighter and permitted this to happen. Evidently, they would need electrical engineers in paradise.

But the impending stroke of midnight still scared Ruben. The appointed time was now only three hours away. How would it happen? Would the ground start shaking when the glass ball reached the bottom? Would it start at one point and work its way around the earth? Would there be live coverage on live television?

In the kitchen Ruben heard his father praying out loud, "Jehovah Dios que estas en los cielos . . ." Was this the end? Was God early? Maybe the elders at the church were off by three hours. Ruben swore he could hear the ground shaking already. He ran to the window and was disappointed. A loud truck was driving down the road next to their trailer park. The end was not there yet.

Ruben let the curtains down and sat back down on his bed. 'What will the new system be like?" he thought to himself. "No more death. No more hunger. No more needs or wants." When it finally came, he and his family would never have to wear that yellow II on his clothes again.

But he could not accept it as that. There were too many questions still unanswered. Too many things that people just accepted on blind faith. Wouldn't we need educated people in the new system? Someone had to build those beautiful homes depicted in the pictures in all of those books and magazines put out by the church. Someone had to grow and harvest all of the fruit the people in the pictures were always eating. Would there be migrant workers in the new system of things? Would God pay better than the $18.50 a day people made now?

And what if people got sick? He had always been taught that they wouldn't, but what if he were to be outside playing baseball with this brother,

Rey, Jr. , and got hit in the head with the baseball? Where would they take him? What if he fell down and skinned his knee? Would it bleed? And if it did bleed, could he die? But the church said there would be no more death. Everyone believed it. There would be no more death. No more pain.

People who were now dead would be brought back to life. That was another teaching. Would that happen at midnight? Would dead people start popping out of their graves at the first stroke of midnight or wait until the last one? If so, what would they look like? He had seen enough scary movies on Saturday afternoons with Freddy Kruger, Jason, and Michael Meyers to know that if 'buelito Chito showed up looking like that, he would scream and run like hell in the other direction.

Ruben heard Eyewitness News start on Channel 5. He knew it must be ten o'clock. Armageddon was surely two hours away now. "It must have already started somewhere in the world," he thought to himself. Why were they not reporting it? The man on T.V. looked calm as he spoke about the New Year celebrations taking place all over the country and all over the world. Surely, he would get a notice any minute now and start talking about the earth swallowing people up and about how the three (or was it four?) horsemen of the apocalypse had just descended from the heavens. The guy on T.V. said the weather was next and broke for a commercial.

Ruben could stand it no longer. The brothers and sisters of the church said it would happen in

2032. And here he was. Living out the last two hours of 2031! When would it start, and how would it end? And would he be one of the chosen ones? Would he be so lucky? He had always read what he was supposed to. He even underlined the answers in the magazines they studied weekly. He knew the faith. He knew what it demanded of him. And he gave it freely.

Then he remembered something. A passage he had read somewhere. The *Bible*? One of the magazines? *El librito azul*, perhaps? It said something like that you could be the most faithful, god-fearing, honest, church-going person in the world, but that even then, God might not even save you. This was not fair, and it frightened Ruben even more. "Even if you do everything you're supposed to," he thought to himself, "He still might not save you."

He reached over to his night stand and grabbed his copy of *The Holy Scriptures*. Maybe if he was holding it, he thought, when Armageddon started, God would save him. He held the book tightly in his hands and prayed silently to himself. He felt his eyes fill with tears and his heart beating loudly in his chest. His fingers ached as he gripped the book even more tightly in his hands. Outside, he heard firecrackers as the neighborhood kids lit up a whole pack of Black Cats. A long series of successive bangs and then quiet.

It was now eleven o'clock. Rey, Jr. had just changed the T.V. back to the celebration in New

York. Ruben could hear people celebrating and singing *Auld Lang Syne*. "Happy New Year 2032!", they said. Were they going to be swallowed up like the church said? Where were all the dead people coming back to life? Was Armageddon late? Was God not punctual?

Ruben nervously put the *Bible* down on his night stand. Could the church have gotten it wrong? They said it would happen in 2032, and 2032 was already here in New York City. And wasn't that where the church's main offices were? Could they have gotten it wrong?

From the window Ruben saw an orange glow. His heart skipped a beat and he ran for his *Bible*. With it gripped tightly in his hands, he approached the window. Slowly he lifted the curtains. The kids from down the block were lighting Roman Candles in the middle of the street. The next ball of fire bathed his face in blue as it ascended into the night sky.

He let the curtain down and sat on his bed for the rest of the hour until midnight reached the valley of Texas. From where he sat he could hear the neighbors celebrating the New Year. A few minutes after midnight, his grip on the *Bible* loosened. There would be no Armageddon tonight, he realized. The people in the church got it wrong. All the fear and worry he had felt had been for nothing. Ruben opened the door to his closet and threw the *Bible* in there. It would be many years before he would once again look inside that thing. He had believed in it so whole-heartedly that he could not even imagine that anyone, especially the brothers and sisters from church, would have gotten it wrong.

From this point on, Ruben grew very skeptical of the church. He came to find out that they foretold the end of the world would happen in 1874, 1914, 1918, 1975, and then again in 2032. As far as Ruben could tell, something he told others many times, we are still here.

Twenty-five years later, Ruben looked back to that scary night in 2031, as he prepared to celebrate the coming new year with his wife. He remembered the fear the church had instilled in him. He thought about the frightening pictures in the books and magazines the church put out. He thought about how he himself had envisioned the total destruction that the church had told him would come in 2032.

As Ruben stood at another turning point in the history of mankind, he came to the realization that the truth can take many forms and has many masters. The truth the church had ingrained in him as a child had changed. The truths he had learned since then remained lucid and difficult to grasp. The truth that he had within him now was that man has little knowledge of when anything, especially the end of the world, is going to happen.

"And those who do," he told himself, "are only fooling themselves and those of believe them." He held his wife tightly in his arms and witnessed the start of the new year.

LA ESPIGA

I close my eyes and remember. From my station along the great wall in which I sit I look back to the days and nights I spent in Eagle Pass. A certain smell touches off a landslide of images and emotions. I remember . . .

It's 2:00 a.m. The bus is waiting for me. When the alarm went off at 1:00 a.m. I could hardly get out of bed, but here I am – ready for another day of working in the fields.

My mother always tells me of the hard times they had to go through when they were first married. She came over as a *mojada* and made her way up to the lettuce fields of Wisconsin where she met my father. It was the summer of 2019 when they met. In June of 2020 my brother was born.

But, oh, the tales she tells of how bad it used to be with the gringos. First they stole our land, now they treat us like animals. They also made so many of our people go back to Mexico in 2027 in what they called "Mission: Wetback." They even sent people to Mexico who had their *papeles*. It didn't matter. Don't ever have anything to do with them, she says.

The bus is waiting for me still. I can smell the exhaust from the diesel engine. It chokes the life from me as it chokes my spirit. As I board this used junk heap, I smell the stench of body odor. People look up at me from where they sit. They clutch their lunch bags as I walk by, fearing that I might attempt to steal them. Some of them wear the yellow II, even on their tathered and dirty clothes. Some do not.

I find a seat and rest my tired body for an hour. The motion of the moving bus jars and wakes me. We pull out of the parking lot at Chato's and make our way north on Ferry Street. The electric power plant on the corner of Ferry and Comal streets passes gently by on my left. I lean to my left as the bus turns right onto Kelso drive.

Graves Elementary School. The memories of this place come back to me when I smell the toasted brown grass of the southwest Texas desert. Onward we go through the darkness, toward the fields.

We make a left turn onto Hillcrest Street and a right onto Bibb. This is where the rich people live, they say. Someday, I want to live here. Perhaps.

The bus makes a left turn onto Main Street and takes us out of town. It makes a left turn onto Highway 57--the road to San Antonio, but really, for us, the road to the fields of Batesville.

TALES FROM THE TORTILLA CURTAIN

I can see the shadowy silhouettes of the *mesquite* and *wisatche* trees as we drive by. Every now and then I see the faint outlines of the *nopales* and their green tunas covered with *espinas*.

Up ahead I see the lights of the *migra*. They always stop us on the way out of town. We slow down to a halt. The *chapulin* comes onboard with his flashlight. He asks each one of us if we are American citizens. Those of us who can speak some semblance of English are fortunate. He is especially cruel to those of us wearing the yellow II symbol. They are easy targets of abuse and cruelty. Those of us who cannot speak English are taken off the bus, regardless of whether we are citizens of this country.

Although born in Mexico, I have learned the gringo's language, and he passes me by. An illegal, looking very much like me is taken off. *Cabrones*, we did not come to your country. Your country came to us.

We arrive at the *labores*. Here we will spend the day and the rest of the week, until the *espiga* season is over. A dusty haze looms over the corn fields as the stalks wave gently in the breeze. It's 6:45 a.m. and the temperature already reaches 100.

Los pushers, drones of the man in charge who make sure everyone is moving at about the same pace, come along and tell each of us which *surco* to take. They set up chairs on the roofs of the buses that brought us here and keep an eye on us with binoculars. The dream of every *espiga* worker is to be a pusher. They get to tell others what to do.

And we begin. I reach up and break the *espiga* off of the first corn stalk, then the next, and the next, and so on, from one to the next in a row of corn stalks that reaches well over a quarter of a mile.

If the heat this morning seemed bad, the heat in here is worse. The humidity from the plants all around me makes breathing difficult. The heat is oppressive. My arms grow tired from being extended over my head all morning. But, we continue.

It is 11:45 a.m., and I think I can see the end of the surco. The lunch I made this morning, four *tacos* of *papas con huevo* inside *tortillas de harina*, sound evermore appealing. I make it to the end of the row and emerge. A pleasant breeze hits my face. A welcome relief from the *orno* I was just in.

I walk toward the sweating, steel gray water container they have for all of us *trabajadores*. I pull a paper cup from the dispenser and fill it with the frigid liquid. I swallow once and feel it cut through my throat like a *machete*. It continues to slice all the way down to my empty stomach. The paper cup sticks to my dry lips as I finish and pull it away.

One of the pushers comes over and tell us that was can take our lunch whenever we want to. At this, other people who had been waiting for the signal emerge from their green limbo.

La comida--what a great relief from the toil of the past five hours. I take the aluminum foil off of one of my tacos and take a bite. I look around and wonder.

Oh, my people. Is this what we have come to? Our Aztec fathers, with their great civilization, look down on us with *coraje*. Our Mayan fathers, with all their great achievements, look down on us with *clamor*. *Nuestra Señora, la Virgen de Guadalupe,* mother to us all, cries out to us with *tristeza* in her voice and *lagrimas* which cascade down her beautiful face. *Virgencita, perdonenos, porque no sabemos lo que hacemos.*

I see the sun shining brutally and omnisciently over the fields of corn. *Tejano* music can be heard softly from the radio of one of the *trabajadores*. We eat. Talk. Dream.

Before long the pushers tell us it's time to get back to work. Those of us who did not finish their *surco* have to go back to where they left off. Those who did are greeted with a new one. The difference on this side of the fields is that they have been recently irrigated and the ground is covered with a dark brown mud.

We go in. With the first step I sink into the *soquete* up to my ankles. The caked mud on my feet weighs heavy with each step, but I push on. Reach. Grab. Break. Reach. Grab. Break. Reach. Grab. Break. And so on.

I hear the screams of a young boy. His mother rustles through the corn stalks to where he is. A *vivora de cascabel* has bitten him. He lies there in shock. She sits there holding him. The pushers make their way to where they are and carry the boy out. The snake is nowhere to be seen.

As they rush the boy out, they scream at us all to continue. We must finish the farmer's work. A panic comes over the *labores*, but we continue, not knowing if the *pinche vivora* will strike at one of us next. But we need the money, so we go on.

It's 4:30 p.m., and I am at the end of another surco. I sense that others are also near the end. We sit and *despistarla* until 5:00 p.m.

At quitting time the buses sound their horn, and the masses emerge. As we all line up to get our $32.50 for the day, the pushers tell us that the boy died. A deep silence falls over everybody. They did all they could, but it was too late. The two brothers and his younger sister begin to cry. The older brother looks at the ground furiously as he tears the damned yellow II symbol from his shirt.

The procession toward our $32.50 continues until we have all been paid for the day. Then we all board the buses. If the stench this morning was bad. The odor now is overwhelming. In the hot Texas summer, these buses lack any sort of air conditioning despite the temperatures which exceed 110 degrees.

We suffer, but we continue.

People talk. Others sleep. The relief is that the day is over. The concern is for the family of the boy. *El chamaco ya esta con Dios y sus angelitos*.

The buses pull into Chato's parking lot. The people get off with their *maletas*. We all wearily make our way home. To sleep until tomorrow at 1:00 a.m.

TALES FROM THE TORTILLA CURTAIN

My recollection is burst by the ringing of the phone on my desk. The familiar smells and sights of that day so long ago fade quickly into my memory. On my wall is a neatly framed remnant of that time – the yellow II symbol that boy tore from his shirt so many years ago. It sits there, behind the glass, as a reminder to me. In my mind, I hear my father's voice: "At least you have a job *que esta* air conditioned."

Memories, thoughts, and dreams all culminate in the here and now and the bitterness and anger are buried deep within my soul. I am where I am now because I am standing on the shoulders of all those who have come before me and who have suffered the great treacheries of the gringos. But, . . . I continue.

CORTEZ, COLORADO

We pulled into Cortez, Colorado as the setting sun bathed the local mountains and rock outcroppings in the hues of pink, purple, and the occasional streak of golden rod. I looked at each restaurant wondering if perhaps that could have been the place. Wondering as a Mexican, or better yet, a Mexican-American, whether I would have been served at these places if the time was July 1, 2022 not July 1, 2062.

It was a tale I had heard repeated many times. At family gatherings. Across the dinner table when cousins, uncles, aunts, mothers, and fathers got together in *Allende, Coahuila* for *el veinti-cuatro, para la Navidad.*

The tale would always start something like this, "We were coming from the potato fields in Idaho. We had been traveling for many hours. We were tired. Hungry. Sleepy. Rosario still had Calin in her arms. Pedro was a young man."

"Calin was crying from hunger, so Rosario

133

asked me to stop in the next town. I saw the sign in the distance. Cortez. We pulled up to the place and I read the word RESTAURANT in white letters on the red sign."

"Pedro got off the car and stretched his legs. I opened the door for Rosario to get out of the car with Calin. We went in. As we entered we felt the cold air from the *aire acondicionado* hit our faces."

"The *gringa* behind the counter just looked at us when we sat down but didn't say anything. We waited. Other people, gringos, came in and sat down, and they were served. We waited. Still more gringos came in and sat down, and they were served."

"*Nomas se nos quedan viendo*," was all Rosario could say.

"Finally the *gringa* came to our table. She stared at the yellow *numero* II that we all had to wear back then. 'We don't serve Mexicans', she said."

This was a story I had heard many times. Why we should not trust the gringos. How they hate us. How they take everything that is ours and make it theirs. I always thought it was damned ironic that this would have happened in a place with not one, but two Spanish names, Cortez and Colorado. And in the county of Montezuma!

But, according to my parents and my uncle, it had. Although I had never been there, I had always wondered what sort of people would do such a thing. More importantly, I wondered if these ideologies still persisted.

TALES FROM THE TORTILLA CURTAIN

After we checked in to our KOA cabin, my wife and I had dinner at a steak and seafood restaurant. We could have eaten at a roadside diner that could have been the site of the original incident, but I was not ready for that yet. Even after so many years, I was not sure I was ready to take that chance. The feelings about this place ran deep. Countless layers of resentment and bitterness after so many years of telling and retelling this story.

As I reviewed the menu, I looked around to see the people sitting close by. The lady in the corner, she looked old enough. Was she the one who worked at the diner so many years ago? I wanted to look at their faces and see if my kind were even welcome in this place.

In my over-educated head, I thought of the various behavioral theories that could explain away what happened. As a hot-blooded Latino, I felt anxious and admittedly nervous about being there. This would explain why I found myself being very polite to the waitress and making sure that I followed the rules of etiquette throughout the meal.

Why was I so nervous? Could it be that I expected to be treated poorly, as my parents had been all those years ago? Was I sitting there looking into people's eyes, searching into their souls, for some hint of racism? Some tendency toward prejudice?

And yet, my life experiences have taught me that people change. As people change, so do communities. People only reflect the ideologies of the time, and a community reflects the principles of its people. This was, after all, some forty years after the incident.

We left the restaurant after our meal and drove around town. It was a pleasant evening. Courteous people. Tourists maybe. But kind. I wondered again if these were the descendants of the racists of forty years ago. I continued my observations but found little evidence. In my mind, I tried to come to grips with this place, and my family's perception of it. My experience now conflicted with their experience then. I was pulled in two different directions.

That night I had a dream. As I tossed and turned through a relatively sleepless night, my mind conjured up something that has been played many times over in numerous variations. A white man in an eternal battle against a Mexican man. Sometimes the white man wins. Sometimes the Mexican man wins. That night the white man left the Mexican man unconscious on the floor. After a few moments, he was helped to his feet, ready to fight another day. In a different manifestation of the dream.

Cultural duality. Two people in one man. Two souls in one mind. Much like the culture of that town. Cortez. Colorado. Mesa Verde. Montezuma. The United States. America.

The morning of the second day we went out to Mesa Verde National Monument. Ancient ruins of people we have barely begun to understand. They left behind a legacy of sophisticated cliff dwellings and artifacts. Standing there in the mid-morning sun, I wondered what these ancient people would have thought about the concept of racism. Did it exist then? Did their society allow for it? What were the principles upon which they based their lives? I am not sure we can ever answer that based on stone walls and pieces of pottery.

The evening of the second day we ate at another local restaurant. Again, I felt apprehensive. The cultural baggage weighed heavily. I wondered as my mind cried out, "We don't serve Mexicans!" But our meal was good. We were treated with respect and dignity. In my mind, in my heart, I felt that I could finally forgive this town for my family's perception of it.

The next morning, I read about riots taking place somewhere in Georgia. They did not want any Mexicans there. According to the pickets signs that appeared in the newspaper, they did not want any "RAZA" in their town. The more things change, the more they stay the same. I wondered if perhaps there was a Mexican child in the very town where those riots were taking place who would be forever scarred by what he saw. How would he be treated there? What sorts of stories would take shape across the tables at their family gatherings?

As I read this, I was reminded about another similar story of one of my best childhood friends who was denied service in a restaurant in Lufkin, Texas in the mid thirties. "We don't serve Mexicans." How that echoes. How deeply it wounds.

ROLANDO J. DIAZ

My wife and I left town that morning. The pilgrimage was over. The circle was closed. Finally, after some 40 years, a member of the Rodriguez family was at last served in Cortez, Colorado. This was indeed a triumph of the spirit but a continuing challenge for us all.

THE HOMECOMING

Friday, November 14, 2037
6:30 a.m.

I sit in my seat on this Friday morning in November, and I look back on all the things I was, am, and will be. The dark marine blue sky beyond the window beckons to me with recollections that do not do justice to the events that have actually taken place in my life. The full moon calls out to me from its appointed place in the heavens. The moon. The circle. The cycle complete. Only now can I understand the completeness of the person I have come to be. Only now can I understand that everything happens for a reason. There is a sign in everything. Even in the most seemingly insignificant of things. As I sit here I think back to the week that has just transpired and remember.

Saturday, November 8, 2037

I arrived in San Antonio that Saturday afternoon at about 1:50 p.m. I wondered if my brother would be there at the gate waiting for me. With my dark gray trench coat on and my lap top computer strapped over my right shoulder I left the plane. The people in front of me walked slowly as congestion developed at the entrance of the gate. I looked up and there he was, my brother, Rick. Standing there with his son, Wesley, beside him.

We picked up the car at Enterprise car rental and drove to *Mi Tierra Café* at the *Mercado* in downtown San Antonio. As we pulled into the second-story parking garage at the Mercado, I looked up to the great mural that had been painted on one of the walls of the Santa Rosa Hospital. This was the place that we had come to so many years before so that the condition of my operations could me monitored and evaluated. My parents had brought me there when I was a child so that doctors could take a look at the scars which were left after the operations were complete. The operations for coccidiomycosis. One scar on my right hand. One scar on my right fore arm. One scar over my right eye. This was the one which would have taken my life if there hadn't been that miracle cure from South America. The one that could not be exposed to direct sunlight. The one which had to be covered up even as it was fed intravenously into my arm.

There was the great mural. Many stories high. Overlooking the *Mercado* section of San Antonio. It carefully depicted the saddened expression of a young Hispanic boy looking down and askance due to his tragedy. Over him stood triumphantly, almost defiantly, an angel. Looking down on the boy with such a passionate tenderness that I could not help but wonder if this whole mural hadn't been done especially for me. I know in my heart of hearts that there are probably many other people who have at one point or another felt exactly the same way about this very vision of grace and goodness. Still, I carry this feeling with me to this very day.

As we entered *Mi Tierra Café*, musicians played the old classical Mexican song, *Por Volver, Volver, Volver* in the background. The smell of authentic Mexican cooking was overwhelming. This was the place that we had come to so many times for so many years. Even my grandfather, "'buelito Chuy", had been a regular here.

"Por volver, volver, volver, a tus brazos otra vez" (To return, return, return, to your arms once again.) they sang.

The waitress came up and took our order. I noticed the yellow II on her apron.

"Un menudo, por favor. ¿Viene con tortillas de maíz?" (One *menudo*, please does it come with corn tortillas?), I asked.

"Sí, señor," she replied. *"¿De tomar?"* (Yes, sir. [What would you like] to drink?)

"Un café" I answered.

"Lleguere hasta donde estes. No se perder. No se perder. Quiero volver, volver, volver." (I will come to where you are. I don't know how to lose. I don't know how to lose. I want to return, return, return.)

She took our order. We talked about the flight and about how Rick's kids were doing. Wesley was selling chocolate bars as a fund raiser for his elementary school.

"Chocolate. Maiz," I thought to myself, " Two of the main foods of our Aztec forefathers." In this environment, they still seemed so strange, and yet so vital and inherent to the life that has evolved here.

Rick's wife, her aunt who came along to make sure she was all right on her drive back to Austin, and Rick's two kids got into Rick's blue van and left. Rick and I got into our rented Geo Metro and made our way to Eagle Pass.

We talked about our lives. How they were going. How we have changed since we were both kids. How Rick still wished he had a time machine so that he could go back and change things that did not work out the way he thought they should have. We played the tape that I bought at *Mi Tierra Café*. It was filled with classical Mexican music. The one that stuck out in my mind was *Las Cuatro Milpas*, a song that recollects how the old homestead has been abandoned. How the fields that were once happy and prosperous are now forgotten and unkempt. How the house of their childhood, once so white and beautiful, is now saddened and alone.

We pulled into Eagle Pass at about 8:00 p.m. that evening. My parents were there waiting at their home in the outskirts of the city. My uncle Chuy and my Aunt Geno (pronounced Heno) were there waiting for us. They had prepared *a carne asada*. Someone had dug a whole in the ground and placed a crudely made grill over it. On it they had placed many pieces of meat and onions. As I got out of the car, I noticed that the one source of illumination over this whole area kept turning itself off. Perhaps some short in its wiring. I approached my mother. As always, she cried when she hugged us both.

My cousin Chuy showed up with his wife. I had always thought he had finished his degree at the University of Texas at Austin when I heard that he had graduated. I was told by my cousin Chuy, Chuy. Jr., himself that he had never graduated from UT. Instead, he had chosen to finish his Associates Degree at Austin Community College and had come home. Another opportunity missed. Another potential leader wasted.

I was surprised that my Uncle Chuy spoke to me about religion. What was more surprising was that he confessed to me that he was feeling that perhaps he had wasted his life in pursuit of his religious convictions.

"I have spoken to lawyers and doctors, Rolando. They have so much more than I have. I look back on my life and wonder what I could have done, " he said.

"Look at your life, Chuy. Look at the family that you have raised. Your three daughters, all of whom are here, your son Chuy, Jr., now happily married. You are indeed a rich man. Do not be worried about this man's wealth or that man's worth. There is your success," I said as I gestured to him family as they ate of the grilled meat, tortillas, and other vegetables that had been provided.

Sunday, November 9, 2037

Mom complained about her stomach pains early that morning. Evidently the meat from the night before had not done her gall stones any good. Early that afternoon, my father took her to the emergency room of the Fort Duncan Medical Center. I had always thought of that place as the Eagle Pass Hospital but I guess they changed the name when I was away. My mother was given tests and other medical exams that took up most of the afternoon.

Rick made the suggestion that we go to *El Indio* while mom and dad waited for the test results. We went and came back in just about forty-five minutes. Mom was still in the emergency room. She was insistent that we go get something to eat. We did.

We drove up Main Street and stopped at Golden Fried Chicken. Funny thing is, the chicken had the same taste that it had so many years before. It still tasted the same even after the passing of some fourteen years. Perpetually the same.

As Rick and I drove around Eagle Pass that Sunday afternoon, we drove by most of the old places that we had known in our childhood. The old Graves Elementary School where we had both attended in the late sixties up to the mid seventies. The old house where we had both spent too many years of our lives. While we were downtown, we drove by the old H.E.B. store. Right there on Main Street.

"Remember that place?" Rick said. Pointing to the grocery store.

"How many times did we walk down here because we did not have a car?" I asked.

"Do you remember what our favorite thing to do was when we finally made it to the store?" he asked.

"The cereal aisle. Mom always called them the same thing. *Chirrios.* I guess that would be Cheerios in English. *Agarren una caja de Chirrios.*"

"Back then they still had all those neat prizes."

Monday, November 10, 2037

I walked into the band hall after all of those years and almost expected to see all of those people still there. Still in their teens. Forever locked into the routines that my memories had given them. And there they were. Over the door to the instrument room hung the first pictures that had been taken when the new band director had arrived. I had always heard that they had hung this picture up in the band hall, and there it was. A group picture in the center. Individual pictures all around. I finally found my picture. There I was, still seventeen years old. Still young enough to be innocent, but old enough to be ambitious.

I stood there looking at the piece of my life and realized that the students who were now calling this band hall their own were not even in kindergarten when these pictures were taken some fourteen years ago. To them, this was just another face upon the wall. Just another one of those unknown abstract faces always looking down at them from another time.

Thursday, November 13, 2037

I stood there at the table at San Antonio College and met with a number of prospective students. A familiar looking Hispanic woman approached. She smiled.

"Did you go to Eagle Pass High School?" she asked.

"Yes, I did." I replied, wondering how she might know this.

"I am Suzie. We were in band together. I played the French horn. I don't know if you remember, but I used to sit next to Sara."

"It's great to see you! How are you doing?" my mind raced back to some old memory. I remembered her. Vaguely. Yes. There she was, only much younger. I had been a Senior when she was a sophomore. Two years apart.

"I'm doing good. I'm here at SAC now in the English Department."

"Are you a staff member there?"

"No, I'm just a work study student. I'm working on my degree."

TALES FROM THE TORTILLA CURTAIN

Friday, November 14, 2037

As I sit in the plane, the stewardess has just announced that they will be serving a complimentary breakfast soon. I sit here remembering all of the things that have happened this week. From the nervous tension I felt at the thought of actually going to recruit at my old high school to the painful fairwells that always come from all of this. I always remember my mother crying passionately every time we say goodbye.

The stewardess comes up with the complimentary breakfast on a white plastic platter. On it are a bowl of Cherry flavored yogurt, a tiny bran muffin, a cup of orange juice, a tiny carton of milk, and of course, a bowl of Cheerios.

"Agarren una caja de Chirrios," I hear my mother say. The circle is complete. Past, present, and future are one.

My mind races back to the Sunday afternoon of the week before, and then goes back even further, to all of those memories of childhood. I look out the window at the cottony clouds below and the sapphire sky above, think of my wife anxiously awaiting my return back in Kearney, and smile.

ATOMIC DISINTEGRATOR REPEATING CAP GUN

The year was 2040. The great wall cast its ominous shadow along sections of Commercial Street in Eagle Pass, Texas. As the agent walked along, he came to the corner and looked across the street to Rexall Drug. The December morning made the arrival of the new toys which had arrived by ground shipment from the warehouse in San Antonio. The agent crossed the street just as the saleslady finished setting up the Christmas display. There it was. What so many children had dreamed about so many times. "The Atomic Disintegrator Repeating Cap Gun." He stared long and hard at the desired object. The saleslady looked up at him and smiled.

The agent's attention was drawn away from the window by the sound of a joyful child. Dressed in humble clothes, with the yellow II prominently displayed on his shirt sleeve, the boy stood pressed against the window, leaning heavily on his crutches. He, too, looked long and hard at the window. The agent immediately recognized the child from the photos he had been shown at the lodge.

"*¡La pistolita, mami!*" he said. "*¡Yo quiero la pistolita!*"

"*Ya vamonos, mijito.*" the mother replied. "*El doctor nos esta esperando.*"

As the mother and child walked away, The agent couldn't help but feel sorry for the little boy. Even as the boy longed for the toy, the mother reminded him of the doctor who awaited them. The agent walked inside the store to see the sales lady shaking her head.

"Poor boy." she said. "It simply breaks my heart to see him wanting that toy."

"Do you know the family?" he asked.

"Yes. I see them walk by to the doctor's office every week. The child is dying of cancer, but the family simply cannot afford the necessary treatment."

"Where is the boy's father?" the agent asked.

"Somewhere in the north. Working. He sends them most of the money he earns, but it is still not enough. They need to take him to the hospitals in San Antonio. They could probably help him there."

"That toy that he was looking at. I'll take it." he said, as he put the money down.

As the agent left the store, he marveled at the boy's plight. This one toy was more valuable to that boy than it would ever be to anyone else. He walked along and came to the office of the doctor who was treating the boy. Through the window he observed as the boy sat patiently next to his mother. Waiting. Waiting for his treatment. Longing for hope. The agent opened the door slowly and walked in. He approached the boy and his mother and smiled.

"Te gusta la pistolita?" he asked.

"¡Mira mami! ¡La pistolita que estaba en la tienda!" the boy said with great enthusiasm.

"Con su permiso, señora. Me gustaria regararle este jugete a su hijo." The agent said.

"Gracias, señor. Usted es muy amable." the mother said.

The agent handed the valuable plaything to the young boy. In his excitement, however, the boy dropped it and it fell crashing to the floor. When the agent picked it up for him, he noticed that a small piece of the plastic handle had chipped off.

"Hay, perdon, señor." the little boy said apologetically.

The agent smiled again and handed it to the boy. *"No tengas cuidado, niño. Todavia trabaja tu pistolita."* he said.

Turning to the boy's mother, the agent reached into the pocket of his overcoat and pulled out a sum of money. *"Señora, su hijo esta muy malito. Necesita llevarlo a San Antonio para que lo curen."*

"Pero como lo puedo llevar, señor." she said. *"Cuesta tanto dinero."*

The agent reached for her hand and in it placed a large sum of money he had received from the other members of the lodge. In his right hand the square and compasses glimmered against the blue stone of the ring *"Con este dinero puede curar a su hijo."*

The boy's mother filled with tears as she realized the amount of money the had just placed in her hand. *"¡Ay, gracias a Dios! ¡Es usted un angel!"* she said as she shook nervously.

When the agent got back to his post, he simply sat in the observation seat and stared blankly at the control panels. He pondered about the significance of what he had just done. All of this from a little toy gun.

PRIZED POSESSIONS

It's there, on Main Street. The old S.H. Kress building. In fact, you can still see the faded sign on the brick wall on the side of the building. It's an old three story building that once had all the grandeur of a department store. In its prime, it must have been the hub of activity in this small community.

We first saw it on our way to Commercial Street that sunny Saturday morning. The grime on the windows of the building did not do justice to the three floors of treasures that awaited inside. The front door opened with a slow yawn, as the place seemed to reach out to us with sublime craving and anticipation. We were soon overwhelmed by the many hard to find items that stacked the shelves. Pieces of every imaginable glassware. Spoons, forks, and knives of every shape and size. Knick knacks whose function only someone with a superb imagination would be able to decipher. One wall was lined with cigar boxes, some worn and crushed,

153

others in mint condition. Cremo cigar boxes, Havana Cigars, etc. All the trappings of Americana.

Behind the counter I noticed a sign that read, "All Transactions Final. All Prices Negotiable." It was a 24 by 36 inch sign with red letters against a yellow background. This was not uncommon. Since everything was used in the store, the last thing the proprietors wanted was for a dissatisfied customer to reconsider a purchase.

The lady in front of us was so happy with her find that she simply took the piece of paper handed to her, which she took to be her credit card receipt, and signed it. At this, the manager came over and asked to speak with her regarding some other opportunities she might want to consider. They proceeded to the back room of the building and closed the door. I thought I heard a muffled shriek, but I assumed he had shown her a much more valued prize than the one then in her possession.

To the left of the cash register, a series of icons let customers know the many kinds of credit cards they accepted. Some I recognized. Others were a bit peculiar for they carried icons that seemed gothic, or at the very least, foreign to me. "Get Now. Pay Later," the sign read. I never liked these schemes. Not then. Certainly not now.

The manager, a rather handsome man with a square jaw, a goatee, dark suit and burgundy tie emerged from the back room and approached us. I noticed that his well-worn name tag read Mr. Sparky Caulderon. It was a Spanish surname, I thought, for I had seen various spellings of the same surname. On his right hand, I noticed a green II tattooed on his index finger. He seemed out of place in this environment, yet he seemed to be a natural part of everything around us.

"Are you looking for anything in particular?" he asked.

"Well," I said, "my wife likes glassware and old Dr Pepper collectibles. I am always on the lookout for 50's era science fiction books."

He courteously walked us to the glass section, where my wife quickly noticed the many fine collectibles that she would love to have. She stayed behind as Mr. Caulderon walked me over to the book section of the store. My, what a collection they had! The original Tom Swift from the early part of the 20th century to the Tom Swift Junior series to Tom Corbett, Space Cadet, to the works of Arthur C. Clark and Isaac Asimov! This was indeed a science fiction collector's paradise!

"Let me know if I can be of any further assistance," he said as he walked away toward another customer.

"Thank you," I replied, as I eyed the many titles in front of me.

Mr. Caulderon approached the perplexed figure of a man who waited patiently for him. In his hands was an elegant leather-bound book. He held it caressingly, as if it was worth more than life itself. His hands shook as he took his eyes from the book and looked deep into the eyes of Mr. Caulderon. For an instant, I thought I sensed the feeling of weary resignation from the man.

"Ah, Mr. Sanchez, I see that you are still here," he said with sincere enthusiasm. As I walked away, I heard the man with the book whisper something unintelligible under his breath. It seemed as if he were pleading with the salesman about renegotiating the deal for the book he had made earlier. Mr. Caulderon simply smiled as he listened to the man make his case.

This place could not be any better. Each author was harder to find than the next. Each title was even more rare than the previous one I looked at. Before long, I found myself holding at least fifteen books. Some had a high monetary value, but not one had a price on it. I was indeed in heaven. It was too good to be true.

With my books in hand, I managed to tear myself away from the shelves and went to look for my wife. I found her in the midst of so much Dr Pepper memorabilia it made my head spin. Salt shakers, bottles from every era, tin signs, posters, lamps, pillows, belt buckles. Basically anything and everything that one could imagine that had been drummed up by some promotional company to help sell the product was there. My wife had taken a hand-held shopping basket and was quickly filling it with these rare finds. The look on her face was euphoric.

I went up to the front counter and asked if I could leave my books there and continue to shop for other items. The lady with the red ear rings behind the counter rather pleasantly told me that it would not be problem at all. She would be happy to safeguard my books until we were ready to check out. She smiled only too pleasantly.

I made my way to the toy section and about fainted when I came across old Hubley Atomic Disintegrator Ray Guns, still in their original boxes, but none of them had a price on them! And they had about ten of them. I had seen these very items sell for as much five hundred dollars in collectors markets across the state! This was still too good to be true!

They even had some of the old Buck Rogers Ray Guns, also in great near-mint condition. I wondered if I should grab all I could and make a dash for the cashier before anyone got their hands on these things. Against what I considered to be my better judgment, I decided to pick up one of each of the toys and continued to seek out other items that were once-in-a-lifetime finds.

I turned the corner to find frames upon frames of autographs. All neatly lined and geometrically balanced along the walls of a room that could have been taken right out of the pages of an old Bijou Theater Magazine. From Abbott and Costello to Laurel and Hardy to Judy Garland to almost all of the current stars of the big screen today. All with certificates of authenticity. None with a price. Amazing. Any one of these autographs would bring a king's ransom anywhere else. But here, they were all for the taking, if indeed the prices were negotiable. It was truly unbelievable.

As I walked around in what amounted to absolute shock at just how much was available in this little antique mall literally in the middle of nowhere, I continued to notice that there were quite a few people in the store now. I hadn't heard them come in, but I must have missed their entrance because I was so excited by the many finds I had made before.

I also noticed that many of these people looked rather tragic. They looked around at the many items on the shelves with little to no interest. On occasion I saw that a few were still excitable about what they were finding, but the majority moved slowly and with very little momentum.

An excitable older woman came up and grabbed me by the arm. She looked deeply into my eyes as if looking for some long forgotten answer. I stared back, puzzled. She reached into her purse and pulled out a small golden figurine of a unicorn.

"Take it!" she said. "I give it to you of my own free will! Please! I don't want it anymore. I don't need it anymore."

"Excuse me?" I replied.

At this, one of the sales clerks came over and pulled the woman away. She struggled against the strong arms of the young man whose attire would have gone unnoticed, except for the red belt he wore.

"Mrs. Castro, please," said the young clerk.

"You know all transactions are final. Now please come with me."

"Don't be greedy! Don't you covet!" she hissed as they took her to the back of the store.

Mr. Caulderon smiled as he approached. "These local folks can be a bit, . . . peculiar, wouldn't you say? They do tend to get attached to their possessions. It always amazes me just how quickly they change their minds. Please, continue to look around. There is so much more to see." He then looked at Mrs. Castro's eyes and stared her down with a look of intense fury. She quietly acquiesced and scurried away from him.

"I don't want it anymore. I want to leave this place," she whispered as she moved. Mr. Caulderon then grabbed her by the arm and escorted her to the lower level of the store. She whimpered as she struggled to keep up with him.

My gut told me that there was something very wrong in this place. I could not quite put my finger on it, but something was certainly amiss. The sales clerks, especially Mr. Caulderon, were only too eager to please. The very items that I had always wanted were all here for the taking. It was too easy. It was almost as if someone or something had read my mind and knew my most heartfelt desires for material things. Somehow they knew about the things, trinkets really, but important to me nonetheless.

I looked for my wife, but she was nowhere to be seen. The section which had only recently been filled with Dr Pepper memorabilia was now filled with something else. I had just left her there only moments before, but now everything was different.

I called out to my wife, but my voice only echoed throughout the building. She did not reply. I ran up to the second floor of the building, but she was not their either. What I did notice, however, was more and more people who seemed to appear out of nowhere. More and more people seemed to be crawling out of the woodwork, and in their hands was a myriad of possessions. Trinkets, worldly possessions, things pined for over a lifetime yet available only here.

I took my possessions and put them back on the shelves where I had found them. The autographs, the space toys, the books. All of them I put back. As I did this, I heard a hiss permeate throughout the store. When I put the last book back and my hands were empty, I heard a distinct rumbling sound coming from the floor below. At this I ran to the stairs leading downward.

I was not sure where exactly I was running to, but I knew my wife was somewhere down there. The sound behind me echoed like a low growl. Like a hound of hell itself. I ran past the many images of people painted on the walls of the store. Their faces were grotesque and misshapen. They were in pain. I swear I even heard their repeated cries in the approaching darkness that was quickly enveloping the store. It could not be night time, however, since my watch told me it was only now 3:00 p.m. The darkness was not the night, but a creation of something else. Something evil.

Up ahead I heard a familiar voice. My wife was calling out for me. This was where she had been taken, not to a private viewing. She cried out to me as I approached the door of her cell.

"Help me!" she said. "They want me to sign, but I will not!" My wife would not move. She would not leave her possessions behind. In her hands were a few trinkets from the levels above. She would not, could not, part with them.

"They are too valuable," she said. "I want them. They mean so very much to me. I can't leave them behind. They said I could have them if I sign this piece of paper."

I knew what the parchment, old and yellowed, meant. One soul for a treasure trove of useless trinkets. You got your heart's desire. The one material thing you most wanted in your entire life, but there was a catch. Mr. Caulderon would claim your soul if you signed on the dotted line.

"Look at me," I said. "You don't need those things. I know that you want them badly, but they can bring neither happiness nor fulfillment. They are just things."

"But, . . ." she said as she looked at her possessions. With tears in her eyes, she let her arms drop to her side. Her prized possessions fell to the floor. The door opened slowly.

"We can leave this place now," I said. "Just leave all that stuff behind and we can walk out of here." I took her hand in mine as we walked up the stairs to the ground floor. At the foot of the steps was Mr. Caulderon.

"Are you both sure we can't interest you in anything?" he asked with a wicked smile.

"No, thank you" I replied. "Now please, move out of our way."

"What are we going to do with these things, anyway?" my wife asked. The front door to the store creaked open. The sun was shining brightly outside. She took my hand in hers. We slowly but deliberately walked out.

Mr. Caulderon looked at us with disdain. He had just lost two customers. Two had gotten away. His thin lips became hair-thin and matched his mustache. Wiping his brow with a red hand kerchief, he walked toward the back of the store. He needed to be with his possessions. All of them.

TRACKS

The sun was beating down on Eagle Pass that spring afternoon. As always, the high temperatures began their cycle at what seemed to be earlier and earlier times each year. It was spring, but it felt like summer. *Febrero loco.* Crazy February. 2039. The thin slivers of cloud were barely visible as they arched across the blue sky. The hot breezes felt warm against our skin.

The four of us left the grounds of the junior high that day. Walked past the yellowed grass and dirt playgrounds of Kennedy Hall and made our way to the tracks. *Chileros*, or sparrows as they are called in English, filled the air with their constant chirping. The smell of *tortillas* enveloped some of the houses as we walked by. The music of Vicente Fernandez reminded us of the tragedies of love and broken hearts. He always cried so convincingly when he sang his songs. Real tears came down his masculine face. *Hombres tambien lloran.* Men also cry.

Chuy was always the smart one. His glasses earned him the name *"Lechusa"*, or owl. Fitting, since he was also a trombone player with the 8th grade band. He and his girlfriend, Elizabeth, from *Quemado*, would stay together for a few more eternities but would break up sometime in high school.

Fernando, or "Fern", was the tallest of all of us. He also lived the closest. He had a blue car that had the neatest way to shift from one gear to another. At the push of a button one could go from park to reverse to drive. He lived on this side of the *arroyo* from Concho Street. He wanted to be an architect when he grew up. Always full of energy and ideas.

Oscar was always the street-wise kid of the group. He lived over on Quarry Street. He would not stay in the band as a clarinet player beyond this year. He was always the one who got the girls. Not the handsomest fellow, but he had the certain "it" that girls found irresistible, but which always eluded the rest of us.

My Mexican birth certificate said my name was Rolando, but the others just called me "Role", the quiet one in the group. I was given to writing and playing the baritone sax even if when I had no music to follow. Scars from my youth over my right hand, arm, and eye always made me the subject of teasing and fights. Kids can be so cruel at such an important stage in a person's life.

As we crossed the street we laughed, ran, and carried on as eighth graders often did in those times.

Before the wall, before the crack outbreaks, before the intense gun violence.

"We'll be graduating from eighth grade soon," Chuy said. "Then it's on to high school." It never dawned on anyone to ask why we had graduation from junior high school. It was perhaps because the educators of the time realized that this would be the only graduation that many of us would ever be a part of. I still have my certificate. Somewhere in the boxes that I have moved with me with each opportunity. With each move up. This would be the only one that Oscar would ever know.

"You guys gonna stay in the band in high school?" Fern asked as be picked up a white rock and threw it down the track, his black and white tennies crunching the white rocks beneath his feet. He was the only one of us who was not in band.

"Nel, ese," Oscar replied. "I just wanna keep my sister from getting pissed at me for wasting so much money on this horn. You know what they say about band members."

Oscar had been in his share of fights in his life. Always trying, but always coming only so close. Still, he carried his clarinet home each day in one hand and his books in the other.

I remember that one of our teachers at Graves Elementary School had challenged him to write something for a contest and Oscar had turned her down. He insisted that if he wrote something, he would naturally win, and so would not even bother. Well, he eventually did write something for that contest, and lo and behold, he won. This was a story that he always took pride in, even years later as he went on to depend more and more on alcohol to get through life.

"Screw that," I broke in. "Who the hell are they to tell us what we can do. I'm gonna stay in the band." I have always been defensive and not very forgiving. Memories of the teasing continue to haunt me to this day. Even as a grown and responsible man, the bitterness and anger at people at the other side of two or three decades remain fresh and alive. As if the incidents had happened five minutes ago, not thirty years ago.

"Me too!" Chuy answered.

Oscar handed Fern his clarinet case and grabbed Chuy's trombone case. He put it on his shoulder as a bazooka. Shooting make-believe missiles at imaginary enemies. He grabbed it by the handle and swung it around. To Chuy's dismay, the rest of the case went flying into the side of the tracks as Oscar held on to what was left in his hand--the handle.

"*Cabrón*, give me that!", Chuy yelled as he snapped the handle from Oscar's hand. He walked to where his trombone lay among the yellowed Johnson grass beside the tracks. He put the handle in his pocket and picked up his trombone.

"Sorry about that, *ese*," Oscar said. "I didn't know it was gonna do that."

Fern handed Oscar back his clarinet. Having only his books to carry, Fern had an easier time balancing himself on the thin railroad tracks as he walked. I just trudged along, since my baritone saxophone was way too heavy to even attempt that high wire act.

Chuy didn't say much to Oscar the rest of the way home. In all the time he had that trombone, he never had that handle reattached. All through high school, he wrapped his arm around that case as he waited outside the band hall for his ride to come.

"What I wanna know, Osc, is what the hell you do to get the chicks!" I asked. " You always have them around you, and me? *Ni las moscas.*"

"You gotta have money," Fern piped in. "Without money, you can't buy them things. When I grow up, I wanna be rich. Maybe work in a bank. Lot's of money."

"Elizabeth tells me that one day we are gonna get married," Chuy said. "I think she's right. *Si Dios quiere.*" Being a devout Catholic, Chuy always put things in terms of whether God would approve or not.

This never happened. After a few more months, Chuy and Elizabeth broke up. The rest of us never really knew why, but they always seemed to avoid each other in high school.

We carried on as we came to the big, orange molasses tanks by the side of the tracks. A thin black ladder curled its way up the side of both tanks. In all the time these tanks had been there, few had ever seen them actually used. However, everyone just knew them as the molasses tanks. No questions asked. A few years later, a kid named

Frankie was found hanging from one of the ladders, apparently the victim of unrequited love. They say the girl he died for was not even moved by his ultimate sacrifice for her.

Fern lived just down the street from the molasses tanks. Left hand side of the street. "I'll see you guys tomorrow," he said. " I think mom is cooking *fideo!*" He kicked up some of the loose dirt as he ran to the front door of his house and was gone.

We crossed the arroyo to Concho Street. This was where Chuy lived. He wrapped his arm around the case of the trombone as best he could and gave Oscar an angry look. "I hope my dad can fix this. *Bueno*, I'll see you tomorrow." He somehow managed to balance his books in one hand and his trombone case in the other and walked toward the chain link fence around his house. The mesquite in his front yard waved in the hot breeze.

Oscar and I walked along the path beside the arroyo, which ran behind Fern's house and beside our house on Comal Street. "You ever wonder, *ese*, what is going to happen to us?" Oscar asked.

"What do you mean?" I replied.

"*Pues*, I mean, we are about to graduate from junior high. *Y luego?*"

"*No se, bato.* I just hope I can get past high school. My mom never made it past fourth grade. My dad never made it past eighth grade. My only *carnal* only made it to ninth grade. I hope I make it past that. *Pero no se*," I said.

168

TALES FROM THE TORTILLA CURTAIN

Oscar and I had been best friends since we were seventh graders. We had had many conversations like this. I opened the gate to our house. Oscar told me that he was going on home. His mom had been giving him a hard time about staying out too much after school. His older sister had even come looking for him a few times at our house. *"Bueno, pues, ay te watcho mañana,"* he said as he walked away. My hands ached from carrying the baritone saxophone all the way from the junior high. I remember standing there breathing in the fragrance from my mother's rose bushes and from her garden. Up the street, I saw Oscar cross Ferry Street and make his way the hill to his house on Quarry.

The future was still a distant concept to us. Far away. For now, we were kids, enjoying life as best we could. Dreaming about what was to come, but never really knowing where our lives would lead us. The passing of the years would see us getting more and more distant.

We got the word one Thanksgiving weekend that Oscar had passed away. I guess he died the way he lived. He was working his shift at his post. That was when the call came. He didn't stay at his post for some reason. They say he ran out to no man's land and was killed by the system. I heard he lived for a few hours after it happened, but he died anyway. They didn't get to him in time.

I remember talking with Fern at Oscar's funeral. We spoke briefly for a few moments and then lost touch again for the next few years.

My father ran into one of Chuy's aunts in Eagle Pass a few years ago. He asked her about Chuy. She said he had died a few years before. Cancer. He was in his early thirties. He had lived in Austin the last time I knew about him. Even came to our wedding. One of the last things I remember about Chuy was that he was doing well working at the local H.E.B. He had even bought himself a really nice diamond ring.

I ran across the Eagle Pass Alumni homepage many years later. Listed there, among the class members of the year we graduated was Fernando. It was a name I had not heard in a long time. He went on to get a degree in architecture, but now works in a bank. He is a well-to-do and respected man in Eagle Pass.

I continue writing about our growing up years in Eagle Pass. I am not sure what will ever happen to these stories, but I feel that it is something I need to do. I see so many students at the college studying about the history of the great wall. So much promise. I only wish that Oscar and Chuy were still here so that they, too, might be witness to some of the things I have seen. For that one brief moment on those tracks back in 2039, all of our lives were intertwined and headed in one direction. We followed the tracks until each one of us, one by one, made our way to our final destination and left the others of us to continue in our journey.

TRIP TO MECHE'S STORE

The sun was shining hot that afternoon. The wind blew softly as the dried up mesquite husks rattled gently to and fro. The very inkling of the great wall was still many years away. The wuisache trees swayed gently in the breeze. Mom was always in her garden outside the house. She had managed to create an Eden even in the hostile environment of Eagle Pass. Banana tree, green carpet grass, rose bushes, palm trees and even a jojube tree, with its tiny apples hanging all around. She walked around with hose in hand, watering all of her plants, thinking about the great things life had blessed her with.

Inside the house Rick and Role sat watching old reruns of Abbott and Costello movies. This one had the two comics in a direct confrontation with Frankenstein, Dracula, and the Wolfman. There in the air conditioned room the two kids enjoyed the black and white antics they saw on the television screen.

Suddenly the door opened and Role stepped out into the heat. He got on his bike and rode over to Meche's store. On the way there, he rode his bike up Comal Street, past the St. Joseph Church and made the first left. After passing Colorado Street, he came to Trinity Street, where Meche's store was.

He got there, leaned his bike against the red brick of the side of the building and opened the rusty Sunbeam Bread screen door. It slammed shut and the noise made Meche come out. Her hair was always in rollers, and her feet were always in slippers. The sound of Cornelio Reyna filled the air, as did the smell of tortillas and carne con papas.

Role stood there on the concrete floor and looked about the store to see where he would begin his quest. *"¿Como esta?"*, Role asked.

"Bien, mijo. ¿Que necesitas?", asked Meche, the gray haired, heavy set lady who owned the store.

In all the time they had lived at 781 Comal Street, Role had always been the one sent to Meche's for any given thing. Mom usually sent him to get her a pack of cigarettes, Salem Lights with Menthol, which sold for a quarter at first, then fifty cents, sometime later.

"¿A como los chicles?", Role said, holding some gum wrapped in blue, red, and yellow.

"A centavo", she answered.

This day, Rick had sent him to get come candy

and other types of snacks. On the dusty shelves were the Cracker Jack boxes, whose contents were usually a brick of carmel corn and peanuts, stuck together because of the heat and humidity of southwest Texas. Other items included Crazy Cow carmel pops, SuperBubble bubble gum, Charms Blowpops, Sugarbabies, Fritos, potato chips, and other such delicacies.

Role picked up two Cracker Jack boxes, some gum, some Sugarbabies, and a bag of Fritos. He also picked up a red and white little waxpaper envelope which contained a fishing game with minute fishes that could be picked up with a little magnetic fishing pole. He also picked up a Star Trek goody box, filled with assorted candy and a few little plastic trinkets. A well-balanced assortment for an afternoon of watching TV.

Role paid for his items and Meche put them in a brown paper bag for him. He rolled up the top of the bag and walked out the door. Holding the bag in one hand he made his way back home, which was about three blocks away on Comal. This was a long ways off, given the treasures in his possession.

He got home and leaned the bike against the side of the house. Happy to soon be getting out of the afternoon heat. He opened the door to find Rick there enjoying the laughs of the movie.

Thus concluded one of the many times when Role was sent to Meche's store. Insignificant little moments that make up a lifetime of memories along the Tortilla Curtain.

A TRIP DOWN
MEMORY LANE

August 2037

I drive down Highway 57 this hot summer night. The rear view mirror reveals nothing but the blackened southwest Texas desert shrouded by the cover of night. The air is warm and dry. Ahead I can see the lights of the city where I grew up. From this distance it looks to be a great city. But even in this, appearances do not match the reality that exists beneath the facade. The great wall cuts through both cities like a great wound that will not heal. I make a right turn onto one of the main roads which lead out of Eagle Pass. The florescent lights from the truck stop at one of the corners at the intersection gives the interior of my car a passing illumination.

And there it is. Eagle Pass. The town where many of the memories which haunt me first came to be. Will I see anyone I know? Will they recognize me? Will they care? I pass Loop 361, which runs from one side of town to the next. In my absence it has been extended to connect with El Indio Road. The old drive-in is not there anymore. The Sonic Drive-In is still open at this late hour. I pull in. The past is here. So am I.

I place the order. Cheeseburger. Plain with mayonnaise only. Fries and a Coke.

It was here that I experienced my first experience with the *escaleros* in a summer which seems so very long ago. I see the images which were faded in my memory become as real as the day I first experienced them.

The past. I see the images of my brother and I as we pull into the restaurant across the parking lot. Park. The truck comes by with those who will soon be our adversaries. The yellow II spray painted on the side. Insults are exchanged by those around me and those who are on that truck. Away they go. A few minutes later they come back. With a few more "friends" than we have. The first punch is thrown and the fight begins.

I call it a fight, but perhaps that is a misnomer. We weren't really part of any gang, at least not as they are known today. We were just out for a night with friends. Unfortunately, the one person who was the cause of this particular incident had a girlfriend who was, shall we say, in a relationship with one of these illegals. It was because of her that the trouble started, and it was because of her that I ended up with two porcelain teeth in my mouth.

Details of the fight? It is nothing spectacular, really. Some *escalero* is beating on my brother so I have to beat on him. I look up to see a huge mountain of a man. His fist makes contact with the lower left side of my face.

Amazing. Every time I ever wrestled or played at fist-fighting with my friends, it was never like this. We could take pretend punches at each other and walk away unscathed. But this is different.

In a flash it is over. The police come and throw my brother and me into the backseat of the car. The members of the other group manage to make their escape. Bastards.

Memories.

The present. My food is here. The tray is left hanging from my window. I take the first bite of it. I look around to see if anyone is looking at me. No one is. All of the people I ever knew in this town are either gone or dead. There is no one left of those who would be my enemies.

I finish my dinner and put the tray on the shelf over the order microphone. I turn the car on, back out, and drive around this place, much like I did so many times way back when. I make a right turn onto Main Street.

Main Street. The main street on which we cruised so many times so many years ago. Here it is. The funny thing is that I see other car loads of people out there. They are doing the same things I used to do. I come to a red light at the corner of Main and Bibb. The grocery store on the corner there used to be a department store. It was burned down in one of the *escalero* riots.

The past. The memories come alive again. We live over on Pecos Street. The bursting of the bullets in their gun shop can be heard from very far away. The next day many people show up to scavenge and loot what is left of the store. I see a half-burned five dollar bill that came from that store. The person who shows it holds it up with pride.

The present. Back to reality. The light turns green. I go straight on Main until I come to Pecos Street. I turn right. After traveling for about a block and a half I see the old and rundown building where I used to live. "Aca el Senior Moreno" is what we always called it. Whenever we referred to that time and place it was, "When we lived *aca el Senior Moreno.*" Interesting.

The past. I see even more images in my mind. We sit and watch the drive-in movies that are shown at the drive-in just down the hill. Unfortunately, we can only hear the movie when the wind blows just right. Otherwise, it is a matter of lip reading.

My dad goes to work for Lance while we are living here. Good job. Secure future. Eagle Pass is an open market for the potato chips, candy, etc. that this company sells. Away he goes.

He always wondered why we never joined any sports like the other kids we knew. Perhaps it was because he was never around to take us to these sporting events. He was always out of town. By the time he realized what was happening, we were already grown. I love my father, but I have never really felt close to him.

The present. Someone behind me honks his horn. He needs to go down the drive way I am presently blocking. I move. He enters. I grin when he walks into the very same building in which I used to live.

I move on. I drive through a couple of streets whose names I have forgotten, make a left turn on Hillcrest and a right turn on Kelso. The elementary school where I spent the formative years of my life comes into view.

The past. The image procession begins anew. I start here in the fall of 2011. (Can it be so long ago? Oh God, how the ghosts from this time have haunted me to this day!) The scars on my right hand, my forearm and over my right eye leave me open to so much humiliation. "Martian," I am called. "Frankenstein, Bionic Eye, Incredible Hulk." Children can be so cruel sometimes.

And yet, it is here that I first develop my love for school. I am so upset when I receive an "I" as a letter grade because I have always received "S"'s before. I really don't understand what the grade means, I just know that the grade of "S" is the one that is the most desired. I see myself working out of *Sally, Dick, and Jane books.* Their ideal lives are so very much different from the one I have ever known. Before long, I start to yearn for the lives these people live. I really don't know that they are fictitious characters. I want to have neat, loving grandparents who live on a farm with a red barn. I want to be able to go to extravagant places like Mount Rushmore or Yosemite National Park on vacation.

I feel the continuing onslaught of emotions. It is here that I have my first fight with some kid whose name I can no longer remember. He is a member of a little gang of kids who picked on me. There I am, trying to do some chin-ups during P.E. class. "Come on, Martian!", he yells. I stop what I am doing and approach him. You know how kids will stand there and exchange insults with their fists clenched and ready. Well, that is how we stand. He doesn't believe I will fight so he puts his fists down. I see my chance. I deck him with my right fist.

The present. I turn the car back on and move on. I make a left turn on Ferry Street and a right turn on Comal Street. I turn the engine off and sit there, staring at the house on 781 Comal. The memories emerge with new life, for this was one of the most important places in my life. How I have dreamed of this place!

The past. This is where I have so many parties with so many friends. The constant hum of the electric power plant on the corner is the only sound. The neighbors are the reason we leave. After the fight with the *escaleros* at the Sonic and the Kentucky Fried Chicken place, things are never the same. Most of our neighbors have either friends or relatives who are illegals and thus on the opposing side of that damned fight from the one we find ourselves on. The ridicule is difficult to handle. My parents sell the house for around fifty thousand.

The present. I arrive at the Eagle Pass Junior High School a little after 11:00 p.m. The whole building is dark. I pull up behind it to where the band hall entrance used to be. I haven't been back there since I left it in 2014. It may still be the band hall. I heard it was remodeled, so things are probably different. I sit there in the darkness, with only my recollections as a stabbing encouragement toward enlightenment.

The past. Puberty is a difficult time for me. Everyone else seems to make the necessary adjustments of adolescence. I am always a little bit behind the rest of the pack. Girls. Oh, boy. What a fun time I have when it comes to girls. I am never blessed with that certain thing that girls find so attractive in boys. Everyone around me seems to have it, though. Much as I lag behind in my physical development, I lag behind in my social assimilation.

I can't express my feelings to others, so I begin to write them down. How pleased I am when I receive a good grade in English class. That is the time when the debates about the building of the great wall is all over the news. I write an essay called "The Golden Opportunity" based on what I know, or think I know, about the whole mess. The English teacher makes some very supportive comments on it. I know this is my calling, so I start to keep journals and time letters which I write to myself one year and read from myself the next.

The funny thing is, I later see that English teacher and she mistakes me for one of the more popular students in my class. The point is that she changes a life with a simple remark that she soon forgets.

It is in junior high that I learn to play the saxophone. Actually, I start with the clarinet. I play it for about a year, then switch over to the baritone sax. I really pick up the lessons and before long, I am playing the saxophone along with the rest of the band.

The present. In the distance I see a police car. I start the car and slowly move on. I make a right turn onto the Del Rio Highway. The drive to the intersection of this highway and the loop is a brief one, and I make a right turn.

I make a right turn on First Street and come to Eagle Pass High School, the pinnacle in the lives of so many of the people I grew up with. These were the years that they have always lived for. This was when they were in their prime. So was I.

The past. I continue playing the saxophone all through high school. I jump around between the baritone sax, the tenor sax, and the alto sax. I finally settle on the tenor. The half-time shows where I play solos in front of the rest of the band are some of the best memories I have from that time.

It is in high school that I discover drama, or at least a semblance of it. I take a beginning Drama course and get hooked. The first scene I am ever in is one from *Dark of the Moon* in which I play the part of John the Witch-boy. As a Senior in high school, I later play the same part in the U.I.L. One Act Play production.

The present. Oh, Eagle Pass. The memories that you hold for me. Not all of them good, but not all of them bad. This is the place where the tapestry of my soul was begun. The experiences that I would later encounter at the various universities I would attend would all draw their power from the emotions and observations that were first planted in this little southwest Texas town.

I start the car and get back on the loop. I make a left turn onto the same highway I took into town. I make left turn on Highway 57. The florescent lights from the truck stop at the corner of the intersection once again illuminate the interior of my car.

I drive on into the darkness. I think of my wife. She is my present and my future. This is my past. Most of the people I remember are gone, but their images will be forever playing within my mind. Those who still live there shall be forever unaware that on this insignificant night, an insignificant fellow was in town to relive the memories.

HASTA LOS POLITICOS APRENDIAN ESPANOL

En aquellos días, mucha gente se ofendía cuando hablábamos nuestro idioma nativo. Siempre pensaban que hablábamos de ellos o que teníamos algo que conducir en secreto. A través de los pasados ochenta o noventa años, mucha de la gente que ha vivido en los Estados Unidos se a tratado de olvidar del español. Muchos no han querido que sus propios hijos e hijas sepan como hablar su propio idioma.

La gran ironía es que en aquel entonces, el español fue una lengua muy importante. Hasta los políticos mismos trataban de hablar algunas palabras en español. George W. Bush, antes de ser

Presidente de los Estados Unidos, estudio español en secundaria y en colegio. Al Gore, Vice Presidente de los Estados Unidos, estudio español a la edad de dieciséis años cuando paso un verano en México. Aunque ningún candidato se consideraba fluente en español, cada uno se aventajo del español en su campaña.

Cada vez que hablaban con la gente hispana, siempre trataban de decir algo en español. Los dos candidatos decían que trataban de hablar español para demostrarle respeto a la comunidad hispana. Pero, mucha gente pensaba que el hablar español no era suficiente. Los dos candidatos tenían que concentrarse en asuntos importantes a la gente hispana, como educación, servicios de salud, crímenes, e inmigración.

Muchos votantes también pensaban que los candidatos se olvidarían de los asuntos importantes al llegar a la casa blanca. Lo importante es que la populación hispana tenía el poder electorado que estaba creciendo más rápido que ningún otro grupo. En aquella fecha, hispanos componían más que cinco por ciento del público votante. California, Texas, Nueva York, y Florida, todos con populaciones hispanas significantes, tenían 144 de los 270 votos electorados necesarios para elegir a alguien al puesto de presidente del país.

"Lo mas que puedan hablar el español, lo mejor," dijo Bruce Buchanan, profesor de ciencia política en la Universidad de Texas en Austin. "Pero, aunque pudieran hablar español con fluencia completa, si los candidatos no tienen una historia de acción o si no soportan las políticas importantes a los hispanos, no van a tener éxito con la comunidad hispana."

Como cambiaron las cosas. Hace tantos años que los votantes en California habían pasado la Proposición 187, una ley que le negaría servicios y educación a gente sospechada de ser inmigrantes ilegales. De por fin, los políticos se dieron cuenta que tan importante y poderoso era el voto latino. Tan importante que hasta ellos mismos trataron de aprender nuestro idioma.

Como dice el dicho, "El que habla un idioma vale por una persona. El que habla dos idiomas vale por dos." Si los políticos mismos se hubieran dado cuenta de la importancia de nuestra comunidad y de nuestro idioma, no los hubiéramos dejado que nos hicieran promesas con intenciones de nunca cumplirlas. Teníamos el voto. Teníamos el poder.

Pero todo eso quedo abajo cuando se construyo la pared grande. El actitud en contra toda la gente hispana parecía un derrame de odio. Tal como existe hoy.

EDUCATION EQUALS EMPOWERMENT

Delivered to the Graduating Class of 2035 in Eagle Pass, Texas.

When I first contemplated the inherent relationship between education and empowerment, I started to reflect on the experiences I had when going through the transition from high school to college. To be quite honest, I had no idea of everything that was involved in getting a college education. In addition to things like making sure that I had a place to stay, enough money for tuition and books, and that I was registered for classes, I had to face issues that are common to many first generation students.

For a first generation high school graduate, these were very important issues indeed. You see, my mother only made it as far of fourth grade. My father only made it as far as sixth grade. My only brother only made it as far as ninth grade. Early on,

I had the idea that I would not only make it past high school, but make it past college as well. The challenge that I had from the start was that I had no one to talk to who could give me advice about how to succeed in college. I would call home and speak with my parents, but they had no frame of reference from which to understand the college experience. Did they understand the process of writing an English paper? Did they know Calculus or Trigonometry? No. The best they could do was to give me general advice about how to behave myself. "Be good, *m'ijo*."

The questions remained, however. How do I get there from here? How do I get my college education if I am the first one, *el primero*, the pioneer, to even think about trying it? How could I achieve success? Where does one start building toward it? What causes people to succeed? I came to find out that leadership is essential to success, but how do we define leadership?

After a few pieces of humble pie, and other such experiences, I came to the realization that most leadership qualities are learned. You can *learn* to be a leader. To do so, however, you have to be secure in and of yourself. Know what your vision is and then develop ways to make it a reality. As a leader, you must also be confident. You cannot be shy and quiet if you are going to lead people. They will turn to you for guidance. You must let your voice be heard loud and clear. As a leader, you must also make mature decisions. Let your experience be your guide and stay clear of decisions that are made in anger or frustration. The best decision is one that is well thought out and made with a clear head and with a strong purpose.

We must also strive to create unity through our decisions. Ultimately, we should all strive to create unity. As leaders, we are here to bring people together, not to tear people apart.

One of my Math professors once told me that there are four types of leaders in the world. There are those who Add, Subtract, Multiply, and Divide. Will you be a leader who adds to the efforts of those around you? Will you add to the organization and the university that you are a part of? Or will you be a leader who subtracts from what others have done? Will you be a leader who multiplies the efforts of others and one who increases the scope of what they have done? Or will you be a leader who divides people? These, then, are the questions that we must keep in mind as we begin to develop our leadership styles and initiatives.

We must always remember that outstanding leaders are, above all, ones who serve. The Servant/Leader philosophy is one that keeps us in contact with the needs of the people whose needs we are trying to address. It also keeps us grounded in the reality of our quest for empowerment.

How do we become empowered? What are the empowerment essentials? First, we need to develop a good sense of self. We need to know who we are as men, women, sons, daughters, Hispanics,

Americans, or whatever we choose to identify with. Self-identity is essential to culture. Many of us have grown up feeling that we are less than when it comes to our culture as *Mexicanos.* The fact is that we have a great treasure inside each and every one of us. We must remain connected to all of the cultures which make us who we are.

Our self-image is also reflected in our language. For those of you who speak a language other than English, I want to strongly recommend that you maintain that language. If you only speak one language now, then you must learn a second or third one. English is the language of empowerment in this country. Learn it. Master it. But we now live in a global society, so you must also keep your other languages alive. If you speak Spanish, Vietnamese, Portuguese, Italian, Arabic, Chinese, or any of the other important languages of the world, be sure that you nurture these skills because they will be a vital part of your future and a vital connection to your culture.

An important thing to remember, however, is that a strong sense of identity means so much more if we continue our empowerment through education. The Hispanic population is currently growing at six times the national average. According to the most recent census, there are now over 100 million Hispanics in the United States of America. We have a spending power of over 120 trillion dollars. But, what good is it to have so many Hispanics in the U.S. if half of us never make it past high school? We need to graduate from high school. Our people need us to do this. Our country needs us to do this. We cannot expect to be powerful by numbers alone. Education and graduation are important to our success.

We also need to graduate from college. We need to count ourselves in the ranks of all of those who have an Associates Degree, a Bachelor's Degree, a Master's Degree, a Doctoral Degree, a Doctorate of Jurisprudence, a Medical Degree, and so on. But do you have what it takes? Do you have the essential element to get through college? Do you have the one thing that will get you through this and many of life's other challenges? What is this all important ingredient to success? *Ganas. Ganas* for Graduation. You should say to yourself, "I want to be there! I want to succeed!" And you must listen to that inner voice that you have deep inside that tells you *"¡Si se puede!"* Let me tell you this, and I want you to remember these words. We have it within ourselves to become more than others think we can accomplish.

The world is a big place. Too many of us think that we have got it all figured out. That we know it all. When this happens, we begin to stagnate. The paradox of getting an education is knowing that the more we know, the more we realize how little we really do know. We must always remain teachable. Always be willing to learn something new, and to see the same old things from a new perspective. We must remain open to all forms of knowledge.

Let me ask you this, how many of you believe that knowledge is power? What would you say if I told you that this is a wrong assumption? In my humble opinion, knowledge is not power. In and of itself, it is next to nothing. What do I mean by this? Applied knowledge is power. We may have a whole encyclopedia in our heads, but if we choose to do nothing with it, it means nothing. It is when we apply what we know that we can attain an education. It is when we apply what we know that we can go beyond whatever challenge life has in store for us. It is when we apply what we now that we can ultimately achieve success.

In closing, then, let me leave you with these thoughts. There are people who accomplish what others only dream of. Some people dream, and that is all they ever do. It is up to you to take full advantage of the opportunities presented to you. Focus on success and you will achieve things that you cannot even begin to imagine right now. *¡El querer es poder!*

DINNER WITH MY GRANDFATHER

It was a cloudy, rainy day when I first arrived in San Antonio that November afternoon. The drive had made me tired and hungry. As I drove through the traffic of the big city, stalled every now and then due to some traffic accident or over zealous driver, I realized that I hadn't eaten since breakfast that morning.

There was one place that quickly came to mind—Mi Tierra Café. This was a place that had so many of my memories from childhood, that I simply had to stop. I continued my drive and came off at the downtown exit. I drove around and doubled back, found the Mercado of San Antonio, and parked the car.

My, how the place had changed since my childhood days. Where once stood a modest business now stood a vastly popular establishment. Customers everywhere. And that smell—Mexican cooking mixed with perfume, sweat, and car exhaust.

As I stood there, I remembered that this was a very favorite place of my grandfather. Buelito Chuy, we called him. *Menudo* was his favorite dish. This I would have, too.

I walked in and the lady in the *China Poblana* dress with the golden blouse seated me. I was reading the menu when I first heard his voice.

"Mijito," the voice called.

I turn around to see if perhaps someone was calling their son or grandson. Nothing. I continued to read the menu.

"Rolito," the voice called.

I looked around to see if there was perhaps another person named Rolando anywhere.

Instantly he appeared at the table. Buelito Chuy, my grandfather. After so many years, I recognized his smile and the sparkle in his eyes. In them, I could see such loving tenderness, and yet a glimmer of mischievousness. He looked around in awe at how much the place had changed. He looked directly into my eyes and realized just how much I had changed.

"Has cambiado mucho, mijo." He said. *"Casi ni te reconocía."*

"Son estos tiempos, buelo. Nos han cambiado a todos."

"You are going to your new job?

"Yes. I received my assignment to Presidio last week."

"Why did you take the job? You have an education. You could do better."

"'buelo, the education I have does not afford me a job that pays well. A degree in the liberal arts has not helped me very much. I have the soul of an artist, but I cannot feed my family."

"You have a good soul, *mi 'jo*. Why must you go and sell it to the government?"

"I have to."

"Can you live with what you are going to have to do? You have read and studied about how bad things are down there."

"Yes, I know what I am walking into. That is why I left my wife and my family back in Kearney, Nebraska. They are safe there. Nobody knows what it is I will do for a living."

"*Mi 'jo*, can you live with yourself? They say people have gone mad when they see the carnage. When the see the bodies. When they realize that these people are no different from us."

"I have been trained, 'buelo. I passed all of the psychological tests. I have been certified as an agent in charge of one of the guard stations. I am fully capable of handling the responsibilities of the position."

"Then why are you talking to me? Why are you talking to a ghost?"

"I don't know."

CEASR CHAVEZ: THE LESSONS OF ONE MAN FOR A GENERATION OF LATINOS IN A NEW MILLENNIUM

(Delivered at the Cesar Chavez statue dedication in Yuma, Arizona in 2034)

The end of the millennium has long since gone. We are now in what many people before us have named "the future." With another thousand years behind us, and another one before us, the questions that we as Latinos must ask ourselves is, "Where are we now?" and "Where do we go from here?"

Today, we stand on the shoulders of the people who have come before us. It is through their accomplishments, sacrifices, and dedication that we have come this far.

One man who sacrificed much and who dedicated his life for the good of us all was Cesar Chavez. This humble man from right here in Yuma, Arizona preached non-violence as a means to bring about social change. Following in the footsteps of other great men like Dr. Martin Luther King and Mahatma Ghandi, Cesar Chavez fought for the human rights of all people, not just farm workers. He dared to take a stand against violations that agricultural producers forced upon farm workers and against the people of the United States who had no idea of the various pesticides that were used in the production of grapes, strawberries, lettuce, and other products.

What does this mean to us today? As we dedicate this statue to his memory, even as we stand in the metaphorical and literal shadow of the great Tortilla Curtain, we must take a look at one of the philosophies that Cesar Chavez put forth to all people. He is quoted as having said, "Once social change begins, it cannot be reversed. You cannot uneducate the person who has learned to read. You cannot humiliate the person who feels pride. And you cannot oppress the people who are not afraid anymore." Because of what he was able to do in his own lifetime, Cesar Chavez has become a source of pride for all Latinos. This message transcends his short life and means as much today as when he first said it in a speech back in 1990. The effects of *La Causa* are as wide-ranging as they are lasting.

We cannot and should not reverse the social change that has come about because of Cesar Chavez. We as Latinos are now the largest ethnic minority population in the United States. Over 94 million strong, we are a force to be reckoned with by the powers who run this nation. In the past we have been referred to as the "sleeping giant". If this is the case, then the giant has awoken. All 94 million of us stand here at the start of this millennium with a renewed sense of purpose and empowerment.

For perhaps the first time in our lives, our eyes are open. Open to the economic power that we possess. Open to the political clout that is ours. Open to the bright future that lies before us.

And yet, we must take pause and reflect on what we learned from Cesar Chavez. There are too many would be Latino leaders who would propose that we as a people should be confrontational and at times downright violent against those who would hinder our prosperity, our development, and our happiness. This is in direct opposition to what Cesar Chavez stood for.

In an interview which appeared in the May 1970 issue of the *Observer*, Cesar Chavez is heralded as an "Apostle of Non-violence." In this interview he really speaks about the sanctity of life and about the importance of doing the right thing when he states,

" . . .we are convinced that non-violence is more important than violence. We are convinced that non-violence supports you if you have a just and moral cause." It was through this strategy that he was able to bring forth the just and moral change that has affected so many of us who grew up in the fields of Texas, California, Arizona, and the other agricultural states.

Cesar Chavez also reminds us of the strength that there is in unity. *"No valemos nada solos,"* he said, *"Juntos valemos mucho."* What this means is that alone, we are worth nothing, but together we are worth so much. This is an important lesson to keep in mind, especially when one considers the great diversity that exists among Hispanics. We may come from 22 different countries, but we are united by our Spanish language and our Catholic religion. We are also brought closer together by the shared experiences that many of us have had in trying to maintain our Hispanic heritage even as we have struggled to succeed within the American way of life. The trials and tribulations of one person become so much more significant if we remember the great numbers of people who have experienced the same thing.

This understanding of the importance of unity, then, leads to empowerment for all people. Even though *La Causa* may have originally been focused on the rights of farm workers, the ramifications of what Cesar Chavez did go beyond any one group. In essence, the unjust treatment of one group directly affects the way of life of the rest. He once stated that, "Society is made up of groups, and as long as the smaller groups do not have the same rights and the same protection as others . . . it is not going to work. Somehow, the guys in power have to be reached by counter power, or through a change in their hearts and minds, or change will not come."

Where are we now, and where do we from here? We as the Latino leaders of the 21st century must take a proactive approach to bring about the change that still needs to take place. Cesar Chavez paved the way for us. Now it is our duty, or moral responsibility, to travel down that road for our own empowerment and for the betterment of generations to come. We must remember that *La Causa* involves us, but includes all people who may be oppressed or who have suffered injustices.

Cesar Chavez understood the sacrifice that comes when a person or group of individuals takes the initiative to bring about change, but he also understood the great reward that comes from helping others. "We can choose to use our lives for others to bring about a better and more just world for our children," he said. "People who make that choice will know hardship and sacrifice. But if you give yourself totally to the non-violent struggle for peace and justice you also find that people give you their hearts and you will never go hungry and never be alone. And in giving of yourself you will discover a whole new life full of meaning and love."

Where are we now, and where do we from here? We must understand that change is not easy, and that we will always be faced with resistance from those who would rather keep things as they are or as they have always been. But, if we are going to succeed in this new millennium, we must continue in our struggle. Those of us in positions of authority or power must realize that we are simply the link to the next generation of Latinos, much as Cesar Chavez was a link for us.

Ultimately, we must continue the momentum that was started by Cesar Chavez. While it is true that each of us has only one life to live, we must remember that one person who stands up against oppression and injustice can make a difference in the lives of many people. "When we are really honest with ourselves we must admit that our lives are all that really belong to us, so it is how we use our lives that determines what kind of men we are," he said. "It is my deepest belief that only by giving life do we find life, that the truest act of courage, the strongest act of manliness, is to sacrifice ourselves for others in a totally non-violent struggle for justice."

Where are we now, and where do we from here? The answers lie in the economic, political, and educational arenas. The solutions lie in how each one of us, Latino or not, goes forth in our personal and professional lives and carry out the dreams and philosophies which will create a better future for all Americans. Cesar Chavez was only one man, but his gifted insight, his dedication, and his sacrifice was for all people.

In an interview with Wendy Goepel, which appeared in Farm Labor, Vol. 1, No. 5 in 1964, Cesar Chavez makes the following statement regarding the state of the Farm Workers Association at the time: "If you look back, we've come a long way; if you look ahead, we have a long way to go." Truer words were never spoken. But, as we begin this next step in our history as Latinos, as Americans, and as global citizens we must remember the importance of action in the face of injustice. Cesar Chavez was one man, but what he did in his lifetime will continue to affect us all in the centuries to come.

BEYOND
STEREOTYPES

On an average day, one has only to watch the nightly news or to read the local newspaper to understand the continuing negative depictions of Hispanics across the state and across the nation. There have been too many recent news stories which depict Hispanics as illegal immigrants who are basically here to take advantage of the system. They are persistently depicted as climbers, or *escaleros*, who have somehow managed to climb the great wall and make a life for themselves at the expense of the rest of the country. There have also been news stories which continually depict Hispanics as drug users and drug dealers. There was even a recent news story which claimed that most immigrants from Mexico are potentially carrying diseases! I shudder to think about the impact that these stereotypes have on the public's perception of Hispanics. We must put an end to these kinds of images being used to tell the rest of society what we are supposedly all about.

Imagine, if you will, that you are from a predominantly white school in a predominantly white community and attend a predominantly white institution of higher learning. Furthermore, imagine that the only exposure that you have ever had regarding the Hispanic community has come from television, motion pictures, or newspapers. What will your immediate perceptions of a Hispanic be? The images that will probably come into your mind will probably be based on all the negative stereotypes that have been perpetuated by the media.

Does anyone remember the Frito Bandito? Back in 1969, the Frito Lay Corporation ran a campaign which warned American consumers about the Frito Bandito who was "cunning, clever, and sneaky." The ads also warned that there might be a Frito Bandito "in your house." If you have never had any connections with a Hispanic, what are you supposed to think when you watch a commercial such as this?

There was a commercial years ago from Pace Picante Sauce. The commercial takes place inside of a refrigerator, and all of the condiments (mustard bottle, ketchup bottle, etc.) are carrying on about how much they are threatened by the new condiment--the bottle of Pace Picante Sauce. There wouldn't be an issue thus far, but soon, one of the characters says the following, "He's coming to take our jobs!" When placed in historical context, it becomes evident why this line is problematic. Salsa is a Mexican product, and Mexicans are already blamed for taking jobs away from Americans.

And then there is the intrepid Juan Valdez. If he grows the "richest coffee in the world," why is he still dressed as a peon and riding around in a burro? One would think that he would be able to afford other modes of transportation. Another image that comes to mind is that of the Mexican leaning up against the saguaro cactus taking a nap. I am not so sure that I would ever even consider doing such a thing.

Still, the images persist. I have often asked people to tell me the images that come into their minds when I say the word "Mexican." The results? "An illegal immigrant. Undocumented worker. Doesn't speak English. Drug dealer. Drug user. Welfare dependent. Gang member. Street fighter. Fat, lazy. Dressed in white, wearing sandals. Bandit with bullets across the chest." The images go on and on.

The tragedy is that on very few occasions has anyone answered with the words, "Professional. Community leader. Immigration officer. Soldier. Merchant. Well-to-do." The irony? That there are so many Hispanic professionals who are vital parts of our thriving communities! Why do they continue to focus on the negative when there are so many examples of individuals who don't even come close to the negative images that are so prevalent in people's minds.

The next time you hear yet another negative Hispanic stereotype, remember the following individuals: Dr. Antonia Novello, the first woman and the first Hispanic Surgeon General, Honorable Maria Echaveste, Deputy Chief of Staff to the President of the United States, Linda Chavez Thompson, Executive Director of the AFL-CIO, Honorable Mickey Ibarra, Assistant to the President and Director of Intergovernmental Affairs, and the Hispanic leaders in your community who are taking the charge in making positive changes at the local and state levels.

There is so much more to any given culture, or set of cultures in this case, than can be captured by a single stale stereotype. Granted, stereotypes do come from somewhere, and there is always a kernel of truth to any given image. Yes, we must report the news as they happen for the sake of the community. But, we must not let these perceptions be the be-all and end-all of what we know about a given group of people. To do so would do a great disservice to that group. To do so would do an even greater disservice to ourselves. Whether we want it to or not, multiculturalism and diversity are here to stay. The challenge that we must overcome is how we perceive those who are different than ourselves.

Finally, there is one more ad campaign that comes to mind. In the midwest, a fast food company named Taco Johns used to run ads with the phrase "There's a whole lot of Mexican going on." The fact is, . . . they are right. The Hispanic population continues to grow at six times the national average. Of this group well over sixty percent are of Mexican ancestry. There *is* a whole lot of Mexican going on, and we are not going to put up with continued negative stereotypes anymore. "Yo quiero . . . Taco Bell?" No. Yo tengo *(I have)*. . .empowerment.

EL CORRIDO DE LA MENDIGA PARED

That damned wall
That Bush put before us--
We still climb it
Or dig under it!
Neither soldiers nor Rangers
Can track us
Because we always
Keep trying.
We search for life and liberty
No matter who is watching
No matter who Bush sends
We have God and His Saints.
No matter who follows
For we only have our lives
Always searching
For a new life and liberty.
Old Grandaddy Bush
Fixes everything through lies

TALES FROM THE TORTILLA CURTAIN

He thinks that in my country
There is no thing as honor.
All of us are here
Knocking at the door
To tell him
Who the real traitor is.
They say the wall
Is a great treachery
From someone that I swear
Once gave it his blessing.
If we can't jump it,
We will fly over it.
If we can't dig under it,
We will plow through it!

¡Esa mendiga pared
Que nos puso Bush
Todavía la brincamos
O la escarbamos!
Nos mandan los soldados y los rinches
A tratar de cuidarnos
Pero nosotros siempre
Seguimos escarbando
Nosotros seguimos por la vida y la libertad
No le hace quien nos cuide
No le hace quien nos mande Bush
Nosotros tenemos a Dios y a los Santos.
No le hace quien nos sigua a nosotros
Porque traemos nomás nuestras vidas
Siempre en busca a una nueva vida

Y la libertad.
El gran viejo Bush
Quiere componer todo a la mentira
Y piensa que en mi patria
No hay gente de honor.
Aquí estamos nosotros
Pa' sonarle la puerta
Para decirle
Quien es realmente el traidor.
Dicen que el muro
Es una gran traición
De alguien quien te juro
Le dio su bendición.
Volando nos vamos!
Entonces escarbamos
Y si no escarbamos
¡La destruiremos!

LENT

So, what's it like to be a Mexican American? Serving as a soldier, as a guard along the Tortilla Curtain? The best I can do is tell you what I perceived.

One time, when my tour of duty was up and I was getting ride from Eagle pass, Texas up to San Antone, perhaps to catch a flight to take me home to Longview, Texas, where I was born and raised. I was a graduate of Pine Tree High School back in 2027. I married a girl also from East Texas, also from Longview. But she graduated from Longview High School in 2030. Met her on a bus coming home from college once. Saw her red hair, and well, since I was one of seven brothers and sisters, I knew that I had to take my opportunity where I saw it. As we drove on, that day when I met her on that bus, I knew she was the one I was going to marry. After I courted her for a while, in 2032 we went ahead and got married. But that's a long time ago. I have two daughters and a son.

But I digress. What does it mean to be a Mexican American working as a guard along the great Tortilla Curtain? To keep people out. To keep your own folks out. Well, I tell ya. It was the year 2057. I got my orders that my tour of duty was up. I got my letter there in the barracks there in Fort Duncan. They told me they were sending a car down to get me. Course, in 2037 them cars hardly looked like cars anymore. They looked more like the early Hummers than anythng, but the funny thing is, I remember it being right before the time of Easter. It was the day before Lent was supposed to start.

They sent this boy. His name was Jesus Rodriguez. Jesus. If I remember correctly, Mexicans and Mexicans Americans are the only folks that name their boys after the Savior. Jesus. He showed up right on time. He helped me load up my things in his vehicle. Whatever mementos I had. Pictures of the family and such. He told me his orders were that he was supposed to get me out to San Antone. It was during the two hour drive from Eagle Pass to the Alamo City, that I found out the most about these folks. Living on the American side. Having to do what they had to do to protect the country, the United States of America, against the very people who gave them their roots, gave them their origins.

I asked him his name when we got on Main Street. That's when he told me the first time that his name was Jesus Rodriguez. Lieutenant. Don't know why they would send an officer to come get me, but I reckon rank had its privileges then. We started up the hill on Main Street, past the long-standing businesses that were along there. Made it past Hillcrest Motel on the left. Past the old McDonald's there. To where Main street veers off to the international bridge with the H.E.B. store on the left and such. Past Eagle Lake right there on the right hand side.

Now, as we traveled in this air conditioned vehicle, I figured I would make some conversation with this young man. I introduced myself. He introduced himself. He told me he was from Del Rio. Graduated from Del Rio High School. Del Rio Rams. Used to beat Eagle Pass High School pretty bad when he was growing up. Used to play Carrizo Springs and even Crystal City, when they still had a high school.

As we turned left on Highway 57, I asked him what it was like to serve. He got deathly quiet for a while. I'm not sure he knew how to react to that. He just looked straight on ahead at the oncoming lines on the road. Finally, he said, "It's hard." For the next several minutes, there was even more dead silence.

Finally, he broke it and he said, "Sir, it's been difficult to confirm the Data System Tracker's requests for confirmation. Orders to kill these people. I know it's for national security, and such, but I just have a hard saying yes to Dusty when I know human lives are at stake.

I asked him what he meant by that. He said that he was a devout Catholic and that he knew deep down in his soul that he was going to spend a long time in Purgatory, if not in Hell, for what he'd had to do.

It's funny. He confided in me and said that since we were one day away from Lent, and since I was retiring and all, that he was going to give up killing people for Lent. When I asked him what he meant by that, he tried to be vague in how he was going to do it. He just said, I'm going to give up killing my own people for Lent. When I asked him how, he just stared straight ahead. That was about the time we came to Check Point Charlie, about fifteen miles outside of Eagle Pass. After they cleared us, we moved on. I wanted to find out what he meant by what he'd just said.

After a while, he said he'd made a deal with his God, and God willing, he would be able to keep his vow that he would not kill anyone. Not any more of those folks trying to cross. He wanted to be true to his faith, to his religion, to his God. He knew that it would cost him his career, if not his own life. For some reason he confided that in me. Honestly, to this day, I have never told anyone.

So, we kept on driving. I asked him what else he was giving up for Lent. He said, "Sir, I think I'm going to give up suffering for Lent." I asked him what he meant by that, and he said, "Well, Sir, I've been trying to balance two ideologies in my head. Am I a Mexican? Am I American? Finally, I am going to try to balance out both. Deep inside my head, I know that I am the conquered. I am the conqueror. Deep inside I know that I am Mexican, but that I am American at the same time. I also know that I have a job to do for my cultures." He stressed that there were two. "For my country." He stressed then that there was only one. "I've got a job to do," he said. "And I intend to do it."

"My roots are Mexican, Latino, Chicano, whatever you want to call it. But my country is American. I've been sitting on the fence for so many years. But I've been living in the hyphen for so many more. But now that Lent is upon us, I intend to end my suffering. I cannot, and will not choose, . . . anymore. I don't want to kill these people anymore, Sir", he said. "I have to reach a balance deep inside of who I am."

He kept on talking like this for the next thirty miles 'til we got to La Pryor. He talked and I listened. He talked about his family. I talked about mine. Talked about where he was going to go in his life. I talked about how I was going to retire in mine. Talked about his high school. I talked about my Pine Tree High School years. Talked about the kids he was going to have. I told him about the three my wife and I had already raised. He asked if I wanted to stop in one of the general stores in La Pryor. Get a soda, go to the bathroom or something. But I said I was fine, so he went right on through.

I asked him to tell me about his family again. His wife was pregnant, he said. He knew that the time would come when his children would ask him what he had done when he was young and worked as a guard along the Tortilla Curtain. He knew he would have to own up to the fact that he had caused the death of so many people. So many people with the same roots, with the same last names, with the same language, with the same heritage. He welled up when he said that he would have to tell them that he had killed to many folks. Men, women, children. That's why, he said, that he was giving it up for Lent.

"I've got to prove to myself, and to my God," he said, "that I'm still a human being. That I am still in God's plan, even though I have had to confirm the death of thousands. To obey the Data System Tracker's orders. Requests."

As we drove past the cotton fields and the corn fields in Batesville, Texas, I asked him also what he wanted to do with his life. He said he wanted to get away from the border. He told me that he had the heart of a poet. He was a painter, an artist. He loved to draw. Pictures of the Big Bend. Pictures of the desert. Pictures of the rolling hills of central Texas. Drawing in any medium he could get his hands on. From pencil to crayons, to water color. It didn't matter. That's what he wanted to do, he said. Maybe set up a studio or a shop somewhere. Explore what nature had left behind. But he hated the color red, he said. He promised never to use it.

We come on the turn off of High Way 57 and got onto IH 35. I told him some of my dreams. To retire in Longview and to perhaps go fishing a lot in some of the lakes in East Texas. Catch some brim, some mud cat. I didn't care. Canal fishing outside of Eagle Pass just didn't compare to the lakes in the piney woods near Gladewater or Marshall.

On IH 35, we headed north. I asked what else he had decided to give up for Lent. He finally confessed that he had also given up lying for Lent. When I asked what he meant by that, he said, "Sir, I've given up lying to myself. For the next forty days, I am going to live up to what my religion has instilled in me all my life. My God told me to value life, for it is indeed sacred. The Ten Commandments told me that I should not kill. Hence, for the next forty days, I'm not going to. I will not lie anymore. At least, not for the next forty days. I'm going to tell the truth to myself whenever a climber or an *escalero* decides to try to cross. I'll find a reason to be lenient. I've got to be. So many have died. I can't live with myself any more. They are me and I am them. I can't live with myself anymore."

We got to the southern part of San Antone, and I asked him if he ever regretted joining the Armed Forces and being assigned to the wall. He said he did, to a point. He loved the pay, since he never went to college. It was good pay. And all the benefits. But he hated what he had to be. "People change, he said, "I've changed. This country has changed. The situation itself has changed. For the next forty days, I will live up to the creed of what I believe."

He dropped me off at Brewster Air Force Base for my hour long flight to Longview. I never saw him again. This was twenty some odd years ago, so I'm sure that his tour of duty is long since over. What I learned from my discussion with this young man over two hours was that Mexican Americans, or Hispanic Americans, whatever they want to be called, are complex people. They really try to live up to their obligations as American citizens, but in the process they are trying to balance their future with their past. Trying to come to grips with both sides of their own identity. Trying to figure out if they can live with the choices they have made. What this young man gave up for Lent so many years ago, many people have given up for the rest of their lives. And yet, so many of this young man's people chose to continue serving and not giving up any part of themselves in one respect. And selling their souls to the devil in another.

Jesus Rodriguez lives in my mind forever. It seems that he was my salvation as I turn back and reflect on my years being a guard on the Wall. I look back on what must have been a terrible conflict within his own soul. This young man was a caring, giving, and ideal representative of his people.

"Vaya con Dios." I said. "Siempre."

DUST TO DUST

There is little hope. I walk about the surface of the earth carrying only the clothes on my back, my sensor unit, and the bit of food in my stomach. The last thing I ate was the rat that was unfortunate enough to be caught in one of my traps. When this whole thing started I had it all--a loving wife, a career which seemed to be headed to great places. Then it happened. It could not be helped, but it was something that anyone with any sort of sensitivity could have foreseen.

When they were first designed they seemed to be the greatest thing to have ever happened to man. They did things faster and better than any man ever could. They were trained to feed us, clothe us, raise our children, wake us up, etc. Why is it that we could not see the great danger that was coming? Or could we? Frank always warned me about making them too damned smart. He said they would take over if we let our guard down. He was right. They needed power, and they found it. The plant in

Waxahachie had only been finished for a few months when the trouble began. The machines tapped into that power and held it in their clutches like a pack of hungry wolves holding an enemy at bay.

And I created you to rule over them all. You, my precious Data Systems Tracker, my loving Dusty. You were to be the one machine which would use fuzzy logic to make your own decisions. And so you did. Now, it is you that I am after. For you are the one who caused all this. I must find you, my child. My creation.

And how you have eluded me. You dumped your memory core from station to station just as I was about to find you. But, my dear child, this is the last network left. Somewhere in the Austin area is your last hiding place. I will find you. My sensor unit will lead me right to you, no matter where you are hiding. I believe you have made an educated choice.

Society as we knew it has been gone for about six months now. By the great miracle of genetic engineering I have been allowed to live. I live despite the radiation which covers the world like a shroud. I feel despite the great suffering I have seen.

I walk toward the ruins of what used to be Austin, Texas. Interstate Highway 35, once the main source of life to and from the great city is pock-marked and broken. Highland Mall is in ruins. There are a few bodies left here and there. Nothing more. I enter the mall to see if I can find something to eat. The upper level is still there, but I can see the gray sky through the broken ceiling of the place.

I look down to see the agonized stares of a woman and her infant child. They were both killed when the great germ warfare was started by those damned things. Here is the price we have come to pay for our own impetuous nature. We dared to think of ourselves as god over these machines we created.

I chuckle. That is the main question isn't it? Did man create God or did God create man? Did man create machine or did machine create man? The great joke is on the human race. Machines can be destroyed, but only man can lose his soul in the process. What do machines care? They don't.

I go into a cafeteria on the first level of this place. I look to see if there is any food left in any of the refrigerators. Why wouldn't there be? I laugh again. I am the only one left. Who else would there be to eat this godforsaken food? No birds. No dogs. Nothing.

The special of the day? Humble pie.

I walk to the university. The green vegetation all along Speedway is still there. Amazing. The only thing that has survived is the vegetation. All animal life is gone. They told me that the experiments they did on me were derived from some vegetable organic source. I guess that was what saved and condemned me. I wonder how long I would live if I didn't have my mission to fulfill? How long can I last without fulfilling my objective?

The university is still here. Most of the buildings survived the blasts that took place before it finally decided to engage in nuclear and then germ warfare with Mexico.

That's the great irony, isn't it? We declared war against the very people from whom we stole this great state of ours in the first place. We have dared to destroy the very culture which has formed the state of Texas.

I go into the Fine Arts Library. Will great literature make any difference now? There is no one to relate it to. Here's a play by William Shakespeare. "But this above all--to thine own self be true." Good advice Polonius. But, I'm afraid that only the ghosts remain of those who would heed your words.

I stand before a great window. From here I can see the university tower. My, how it used to burn orange when our teams won their respective sports. My, how it burned orange and red against the smoky sky when it all happened.

I walk down the main drag. There are a few corpses here and there. Where have all the students gone? Why can't I go with them? But no. I am here to stay, at least until . . . . Guadalupe Street was always a hub of activity, but now it lies in ruins. A cemetery, that's what it is. A graveyard of our past and of our future.

As I walk along Martin Luther King, Jr. Blvd., I think of what the great man once said. He had a dream but died before he could see it come true. I have had many dreams in my life, but I, too, will surely die before any of them can come true.

My sensor unit beeps in recognition of its master. I have found you!! After all this time of looking for you across the great state of Texas, I have found you. You tapped into the power of the super collider, you son of a bitch, and how you grew after that. Unlimited power at your disposal. And how well you wielded it!

I open a manhole cover and make my way down into the catacombs which are like a maze beneath the university. I can sense that I am near to my ultimate destiny. I seek. I search for the answer and the end. There you are you bastard. I knew I'd find you eventually. What? Are you surprised to see that one human has dared to survive your plan?

No, I will not read the message on your screen. And by the time your orders are carried out, there will be nothing left of your central computer network. How I loved you when you were born. Like a parent I caressed you into existence. Like an errant child you developed far beyond anything I could ever have imagined. So now, my child, the end is here. Hopefully somewhere at the other end of the world there is a colony of humans who will not make the mistakes we made when we reached this point along the evolutionary scale.

I search for the auto-destruct button. I begin the sequence that only I have ever known. How proper it seems! It will take a machine to destroy this machine. My how the lights flicker in their place.

Like a Christmas tree. The final sequence begins. I kiss the hard metal surface of the computer. It feels cold to my lips. In mere moments all that I have ever known will be no more.

So long, my child. Sweet dreams.

THEY FINALLY GOT WHAT THEY WANTED

It had been long enough that the illegals had stopped coming. As time went on there were fewer and fewer reports of people trying to cross illegally. The Data Systems Tracker became used less and less. It almost became a myth. At some ports Brownsville, Laredo, Eagle Pass, Del Rio, Presidio, El Paso, and on into the rest of the southwest states. It came to a point that many Hispanics refused to work at the wall in any capacity. Especially in the clean up crews. There had been so much gossip; so many rumors that people had always seen ghosts of those who had died.

The Mexicans being a superstitious lot by nature and their descendants, the Mexican Americans, brought these traits over with them. They, too, were superstitious. They, too, were afraid of the spirits, of the ghosts, of the things they could not explain. Rumor had it that many times the guards along the wall would simply go insane from what they would see in the monitors. What they would hear. What they would feel.

It was next to impossible for any people not to feel any sort of remorse or regret regarding what the job was. The very wall itself has worked too well. More people decided that they simply could not and would not go work in any capacity. This was the year 2130. It had been about one hundred years since the wall had been created.

The Mexicans on their side has simply stopped trying. They didn't care to come to the United States. They had found their own way. Found their own prosperity. Their own meaning of success.

Meanwhile, the United Stated continued to stagnate in its own putrid state. There was nothing happening here. No infusion of culture. No infusion of language. No infusion of ideas. The United States of America stagnated.

They say great civilizations rise and fall. The Romans experienced it. The Mayans, the Aztecs, experienced it. Many others did before. And probably many more unknown civilizations full of their own worth had traveled down this road. Now it was time for the Americans to experience it as well.

At first the wall had seemed a great idea. But it was what it came to represent that was the final nail in the coffin for American society. The world saw it as a great curtain, a great veil of secrecy. The

United States had expected the rest of the world to know its culture, its language, its customs. But, in the process it had shut itself off. It had removed itself from the very neighborhood, from the very society that it had wanted to dominate, control, and ultimately be a part of.

But it remained isolated. It remained in a state where the status quo remained. At first it seemed that the rest of the world would follow their lead, their example. Now in the year 2130, there were very few countries that followed the United States. England had long since abandoned its bastard step-child. Canada had long since cut off the United States, even if it was its neighbor to the south.

Mexico had finally developed and prospered to the point that it could keep its citizens fed and educated. They developed their own industries. They developed their own sense of pride and identity. The United States to the north began to rot in its own ideas, its own arrogance, its own egocentrism, and ultimately its own xenophobia.

The finally got what they wanted. Everyone spoke one language. Everyone there knew one culture. Everyone knew one way of doing things. Everyone became the same.

An interesting comparison – the Great Tortilla Curtain was built by the very people it was designed to imprison. At first, it seemed that the wall was indeed very effective in keeping out illegals and any others who would even contemplate entering the country. As time went by, people started to realize that it was not keeping people out. It was, in fact, keeping people in.

So the idea of the founding fathers, though bastardized in translation, E Pluribus Unum, finally happened. Many became one. Out of many cultures, one was created. And it was the one culture that ultimately . . . failed.

A MATTER OF
ATONEMENT

The water level of the Rio Grande was lower than usual that day. Perhaps the Amistad Dam hadn't let out enough water. I don't know. As I stood on the Mexican side of the river looking at the great majesty of the wall, I wondered about my journey into the wondrous and wealthy country known as the United States of America.

I sat there. Wondering. Dreaming about the possibilities and opportunities to come. The sun was setting. The sky was filled with orange, purple and black. The great wall was bathed in a golden shade of orange. I could smell the musty water of the river. When the spectacle of dusk was finally over, I got in the water. With my life's earnings packed away, I started swimming to the other side.

My cousin, Sandra, and her husband, Luis, always told me to be careful with the undertow. It really hadn't crossed my mind until then. There.

Somewhere between the two countries, I felt a swirl of water come up from beneath me and pull me under. How I wished I'd listened to the advice my cousin had offered! I tasted the musty water. I vainly tried every means I could think of to stay afloat. In that moment of panic I tried them all. The last thing I remember was thinking of all the dreams I'd had.

I came to on the bank of the river. The American side. I looked up to see the looming grandeur of the great wall. The sun was high in the sky, so it must have been around noon. I awoke to see the sparkle of a strange jewel embedded in the mud of the riverbank. It just lay there. Almost beckoning me to it.

I approached it. I picked it up with one hand and washed it in the water of the river. It couldn't have been a broken piece of glass. There was something almost supernatural about it.

I rinsed it again in the water of the river, and it attained an even greater shine.

By now, dear reader, you may be wondering how someone with my background could possibly be narrating this story. In English at that! Well, this was no ordinary object I had stumbled upon. To this day, I don't know if it was a religious or scientific artifact. Perhaps I never will.

Anyway, I stood there, mesmerized by my treasure. This truly was the land of opportunity! I remember putting it in my pocket and beginning the climb. Inch by inch I crawled. Finally, I pulled myself over the top of the wall. Behind me I could see the ruins of Piedras Negras. Before me lay the riches of *Los Estados Unidos.* The jewel filled me with energy as I started down the other side.

Before me was the link fence I had heard so much about. The decomposing carcasses of human beings were scattered all over. I remember stepping on their broken bodies as I made it past the mine field. The five mile run and those damned lasers were my next obstacle. I started running. Perhaps if I moved fast enough I'd make it. Perhaps just this once, something right would happen in my life. I heard *"el sumbido de la luz"* and panicked. I reached for my jewel and held it up to the heavens. Pleading. Bargaining. The ravings of a madman. I pleaded to be taken from there. Oh, if I could only be a white man, knowing all that a white man knows! Having all that a white man has! The whining sound of the laser cannon was the last thing I heard.

That's when the transformation occurred. From that moment on, my life would be forever changed. I came to in a bed of tall *carrizos.* They practically hid me from view. I had, however, been spotted by a border patrol person.

From his position beside his vehicle the patrolman called me out. He was a white man. Gringo. About six feet tall. Dressed in the traditional green uniform, the reason they were known as *chapulines,* or grasshoppers, to my people. He spoke to me in Spanish. I understood what he meant, but now the language sounded so foreign to me. He tried reasoning with me and then rudely informed me that he was armed.

I stood up.

He stood there, as bewildered as I was.

"American citizen?" he asked.

"Excuse me?" I mumbled.

English! I spoke English to this man! I had never even taken a class in my own language, let alone English! Yet here I was, speaking the language of opportunity. I had always heard that if you could speak English, many opportunities would open themselves to you.

"Are you an American citizen?" he asked again.

"Yes?" I replied nervously.

"What are you doing out here? This place is off limits to American citizens. Don't you realize how much danger you are in?"

"Well, I . . ."

I reached around and found a wallet in my back pocket. The strange sequence of events which had begun with the sparkling jewel continued to create things for me. I handed him the wallet. He took it and opened it quickly. He stared at the picture on the identification card and looked up at me. How could I have any sort of identification? My application for a green card had been denied. I had my birth certificate tucked away, but that was all. He folded up the wallet and returned it to me slowly.

I looked down and noticed that I was dressed in blue jeans, a sort of button down shirt, and some sort of hiking shoes. What had happened to me?

Why was this man treating me so kindly? I opened up the wallet and looked at the picture on the card. It was the picture of an Anglo man, yet the features looked remarkably familiar. The name read Roger Fields. The address was 2830 Lawrence St., Eagle Pass, Texas. Roger Fields. That was my name and yet it wasn't. My real name I knew to be Rogelio Labores, but it had been translated somehow.

"Get in the car," he said, "I need to get you out of the danger zone. I thought fer sure you were one of them climbers that always tries to get by the security wall. Good thing you're one of us."

"One of you," I thought, "how could I possibly be one of you?" Why was this man treating me this way? Was it some sort of trick? The last thing I remembered was *"el sumbido de la luz"*, but now here I was.

As I opened the door to his vehicle, I noticed a peculiar reflection on the side door. The skin. The color. It wasn't the sunbaked brown I was so familiar with. It was fair. Pink. The color of the people I had always been taught to hate. I approached the side mirror. My reflection scared and excited me at the same time.

Through some divine intervention my outward appearance had been altered! My hair was not black anymore, but a sort of light brown. My eyes were blue, not brown. My native language had been replaced by English, and an elevated form of English at that! My would-be captor broke my trance.

"This is seventeen, Dusty. This here's a 10-16. Just another one of our people wandered in where they wasn't supposed to be. I'm going back into town. Over."

"Roger seventeen Charlie. Over and out."

The air conditioning inside his vehicle was a welcome relief to the hot Texas summer. All the way back I sat in utter amazement at my situation. When we got into town, he dropped me off at the corner of Main and Commercial. I stood there in Front of Zale's Jeweler's wondering and stupefied. The diamond rings sparkled at me from their place on the window display.

An old Hispanic woman walked toward me. I tried to greet her with the salutation appropriate for the occasion, but the Spanish that left my mouth was not the same as the one I had always known. It sounded just like all the gringos that I had ever heard trying to speak Spanish. She avoided me and scurried away from me quickly.

Was I now to be estranged by my own people? More was to follow.

I reached into my pocket and pulled out the wallet that had materialized there. It was my picture on the identification card. But despite the differences, it was still my face. My features, eyes, nose, mouth, chin. Only the color was different.

The smell of fast food reminded me of how long it had been since my last meal. I looked to see if there was any money in the wallet, and noticed a thick wad of hundred-dollar bills.

TALES FROM THE TORTILLA CURTAIN

There must have been a few thousand dollars in there. I quickly put it away and crossed the street.

On the door to Newberry's Department Store I saw my reflection again. My shoes, jeans, and shirt were clean. My hair was combed. I walked in. The cafeteria was at the far right section of the store. I walked up to the bar and sat on a stool beside other Hispanic men about my age. They turned to speak to me.

"Buenas tardes."

"Buenas tardes."

I tried to return the greeting in the same regional dialect, but what emanated from my mouth sounded so much like text book Spanish. They smiled and turned to the waitress who was there to attend us. She was a well-built woman, not fat by any means, just full-figured and attractive. Her short, straight, black hair was held back by a brad of some sort. Her waitress outfit showed the sign of wear and tear but was still somewhat immaculate. She ignored the two people who had been there before me and came straight to where I was.

"May I help you" she asked.

"I think they were here first."

"No, you were here first."

Interestingly, the two men beside me weren't all that bothered by this woman's actions. They just waited patiently, as if their lot in life was to be perpetually waiting for others to get their chance before they could get theirs. On their shirts I noticed an old and faded "II" symbol in yellow.

"Really", I said. "You need to take their order first.

"What the hell do you care about whose order I take first?" she asked. "They're just climbers and they know it. Besides, they don't even know what I'm saying. They're too *pendejos*."

At this I reached into my pocket and pulled out a one-hundred dollar bill and put it into the hand of the man sitting next to me.

"Do you understand me?" I asked.

He nodded.

"Eat whatever you want. I will pay for it. Here's the money." I said.

I glared at the woman behind the counter then found my way out of the department store and onto the busy sidewalk.

What was happening to me? One-hundred dollars was a fortune in pesos, and here I was giving it away. I wandered up Main Street still bewildered by my transformation. I passed the downtown H.E.B. grocery store. A block later I found myself staring at the movie stills of the coming attractions at the Aztec Theater. I took out my wallet and looked at the identification card.

"2730 Lawrence St." I mumbled.

I asked an Anglo couple who was walking by if they knew where Lawrence Street was. They smiled graciously and informed me that it was at the top of Main Street. All I had to do was to follow Main Street all the way up the hill until I came to the Main Street/Lawrence intersection. I started walking. If the address did exist, what would I find when I got there?

The house was modest, but comfortable. It was on what appeared to be two lots of land. There was a variety of vegetation on the property, some of which I didn't recognize.

Had the force, the intelligence which transformed me also given me the material background from which to enjoy my new-found race? Was it even now directing my every footstep? Had I spent the previous twenty-four years of my life only dreaming that I was a poor, land-working Mexican from Allende, Coahuila? So many questions, and they were about to be answered.

The door was unlocked. I went in. All of the normal furniture for the standard American home had been provided for. There was one room, however, to which I was instantly drawn. Behind a mahogany door was a room full of books which contained the essence of the American culture. I walked in and closed the door behind me. After picking up a book titled *The Essence of the American Dream*, I sat at the desk at the far left corner of the room. I sat there, open book in front of me and, of course, passed out. It was then that I had the explanation of the recent events in my life.

I woke up in what appeared to be some sort of examination table. The beings which surrounded me seemed to have no nationality which I could recognize. They were neither Anglo nor Hispanic, yet they contained the essence of each race.

"Roger, can you here me?" one of them asked.

"Yes." I replied. "But where am I. Who are you?"

"Who we are in unimportant. Who you are is." he said.

"What has happened to me? Everything is different."

"You are taking part in a great movement. The race that we have become is the result of your efforts. You may not be able to comprehend this, but we are your children. We have been for many generations now."

"My children? How can that be? I'm not even married."

"You will be," he said, grabbing some sort of electronic device and making some sort of calculations with it. "You must be conditioned to assimilate to the culture into which you will be sent. Your background must be enhanced to not only contain the sum total of the Mexican culture, which you already know, but the sum total of the American culture which you will assimilate."

"Wait!" I pleaded. "I don't understand."

Before I could continue, I passed out again.

My head was filled with such a dearth of information that to even attempt to describe it here would be but a pale description of a wondrous experience. In any event, this is how I came to understand the references to places, things, philosophies, and ideas which are the foundation of this culture.

I came to on the examination table again. The first face I saw was that of the creature to which I had spoken earlier.

"How do you feel?" he asked, shining a light in examination of my dilated pupils.

"Enlightened." I answered.

"Now you may ask any question you wish." he said as he helped me to sit up. "If you had been allowed to ask any questions before your assimilation, you would never have understood the answers."

"Tell me." I said. "Where am I?"

"You are in the future. This is the year 3027. The world you remember has evolved into what you see before you."

"What matter of creature are you? What race?"

"I am a human man. Of the human race."

"What culture are you from? What nationality? You seem to be Anglo, yet Black, yet Brown, and to contain all and yet none of the specific features of the different races."

"I am all, and I am none. In the thousand years that have passed since your time, all of the races have combined to create the people you see before you now. So in effect, we are one race--Human."

"Are there any national boundaries, then?"

"Only the boundaries of the imagination. The land masses are still recognizable by your standards, but we live as one race, inhabiting one planet."

"You said I am to take part in a great movement. What did you mean?"

"You are the first of your kind. We have given you the outward appearance of a white man, but your genetic make-up remains that of a Hispanic."

"Then why have I been transformed?"

"History has shown that the society of your time does not easily accept marriages between the races. It is your purpose to go forth and marry into the dominant race and begin the process of combining the races into a whole."

"Why me? Why not someone from Africa, or Asia, or any other place?"

"You are the first. There will be many others. We have waited until your time because it is now that the conditions are right for the mixing of the races. We have picked individuals who would have other wise have little to offer to society and made them the saviors of it."

"But can you be sure that you are doing the right thing?"

"Just as we are able to go backward in time we are able to go into the future. We do this now because our future dictates that it must be so. This is the point along the continuum when we are supposed to go back in time and begin the process of the unification of the races."

"Then my purpose is to marry a person from a race other than my own and to eventually have children? Is this the price for the luxury you have afforded me?"

He nodded.

"What if I wish to marry into my own race?"

"They will not accept you. You are an outsider now. Even though your command of your own Spanish dialect has been returned to you, you will never again be truly accepted into the Mexican culture. You will be called a *gavacho*, a *gringo*, or at best, a *pocho*."

"My people will not abandon me. They are not as prejudiced as you make them out to be. Let me prove it to you."

He walked to the console and made a few calculations. A look of surprise came over him. He smiled and walked over to me.

"Very well." he said. "Let us test your theory."

He put an instrument to my forehead, and I passed out. I came to on one of the backstreets in Piedras Negras. The jewel appeared in the palm of my right hand. It had been no dream. I proceeded to the area where I knew my relatives lived. I had only that morning joined them for a breakfast of tortillas and frijoles.

Their house was filthy on the outside. A film of dirt covered every perceivable object on their property. Even the *mesquite* and the *jojube* trees were overburdened by the residue of the environment. Barefooted children played marbles, *canicas* to them, and screamed excitedly at each vain perception of victory.

They stopped what they were doing as I approached. They stared at me as if were a creature from some far off world. They stood in silence.

Finally, one of them spoke. *"Mama! Aqui los*

busca algien!" (Someone is looking for you!)

From the inside of the house I heard my cousin, Sandra. *"Quien es?" (Who is it?)*

The child answered quickly. *"¡Es un gringo!" (It is a white man!)*

Can you imagine that? He was referring to me as a *gringo*! I had become a member of the Mexican's most hated race. My own people cast me out. And yet, I thought I might perhaps explain to them that it was me, their own flesh and blood, who had returned. But that was just it.

The blood, with all its DNA, with all its chromosomes, with all its genetic information had remained the same. It was the color of the flesh that was different.

Speaking the *norteño* Spanish dialect, now that it had been returned to me, I approached the house and knocked at the door. The children simply stood there, glaring at this stranger who dared to knock at their door. Sandra came to the door.

"Hello, Sandra. The most amazing thing has happened to me. I have . . . "

"Who are you? What do you want?"

"I am Rogelio Labores."

"My cousin Rogelio was drowned yesterday. They are still looking for his body." she said coldly.

"I am Rogelio. Don't you understand?"

She backed away from the door and called her husband, Luis. He stood in front of her
and looked at me menacingly.

"I don't know what you want, but you are not

wanted here." he said.

"Luis! Don't you know me? I am Rogelio!"

He threw open the door and pushed me back.

"You better leave. Now!"

I knew there was little I could do to convince him of my identity. I backed off and walked away. The next moments were a blur. Everywhere I went, people failed to even acknowledge me. I couldn't do a thing to convince them that I was one of their own. Hatred filled their eyes every time I approached any one of them.

I felt the jewel in my hand. I knew that my own culture would never again have me back. I was dead to them now. I then bid good-bye to the culture that bore me and wished to be taken away to the other side of the great wall.

I appeared in the great country of the United States of America. Eagle Pass. The house on Lawrence Street was still there. I opened the front door to find the creature from the future waiting there for me. He had two suitcases in front of him.

"You must leave Eagle Pass now. These are but a few things which you will need in the fulfillment of your destiny. The jewel is yours to keep. It will serve to remind you of what you must become. It will also serve as a monitor for us, in case you are ever in any great need of our help."

"But if you are from the future, wouldn't you know what will happen?"

"Nothing" he said, "is set in stone. The potential variables are many."

At this he disappeared, probably into the future. I took the suitcases and loaded them into the car I had been given. My destiny, then, was to move toward a world-wide assimilation of all cultures. I would eventually marry into the dominant race of this country and begin the process of true desegregation.

I left Eagle Pass that day, and headed north on Highway 57, then north on I.H. 35. North to the land of opportunity. North to the land of cultural diversity. North to the place, to the time, to the situation in which all people would live as one, as per the need of someone in the distant future.

I FLY

I fly.
To great and distant lands I fly.
In the mists of the night I fly.
From meridian heights I fly.
I seek.
I travel.
The wind in my hair.
No boundaries.
The map meaningless.
I fly.
I look down.
The wall a distant memory.
I look up
The universe a kind and beckoning friend.
I fly.
To distant lands.
I fly.
Always moving.
Always hoping.
Always caring.

I fly.
Carrying with me the hopes of others.
Carrying with me the dreams of myself.
Carrying with me the prayers of those who cannot.
I fly.
Always.

EPILOGUE

Ha llegado el tiempo cuando nos tenemos que preguntar si nuestro pasado va a tener tanto que ver con nuestro futuro. La gente dice que el pasado siempre afecta al futuro, pero pienso que el pasado no es nada mas que el pasado, y que el futuro empieza ahora. La próxima vez que alguien te diga que el pasado siempre te va a seguir, contéstale que el futuro siempre te va a esperar con brazos abiertos.

The moment has come when we must ask ourselves if our past is going to have any impact on our future. People say that the past always impacts the future, but I think that the past is nothing more than the past, and that the future begins now. The next time someone tells you that the past will always follow you, tell them that the future will always wait for you with open arms.

ACROSS TIME: A TRAVÉS DEL TIEMPO

PROLOGUE

The following is a brief history about how things have happened . . .this time.

Jose and Maria Díaz met while working in the beet fields in Wisconsin. She was there as an illegal alien. Jose, having been born in Eagle Pass, Texas, has always been an American citizen. They were married in 1960. On June 21, 1961, Ricardo Diaz, known as Rick in these stories, was born. Some time between March of 1962 and December of 1963, Edward was born. However, because of complications at birth, Edward died after only having lived about four hours. On September 22, 1964, Rolando Josué Diaz, known as Role in these stories, was born.

At the age of one-and-a-half, Role contracted what has been identified as coccidiomycosis. Although it usually strikes adults in the lungs, it struck Role in the right had and progressed to the upper forearm and over the right eye. Although he was eventually cured, he was forced to spend nine months in a hospital in Phoenix, Arizona. Because of the state of medicine of the time, Role was left with a scorpion-shaped scar on his right hand, a centipede-shaped scar on his upper forearm, and a right eyelid which is not even with the left eyelid. As one of the stories attests, this made for some difficult times for Role when he was in his formative years.

Rick was almost killed by an truck when he was still a child. Although the truck never actually made contact, he received quite a shock from the experience itself. From what Maria has always maintained, every sort of test was run to make sure that Rick was all right.

Both Rick and Role attended Graves Elementary School. There they experienced many of the common things kids of that age group experience. Rick's best friend came to be Sammy. They would remain friends until sometime in the late seventies, when Sammy was killed in a motorcycle accident.

During the middle to late seventies, Rick and Role worked in the fields of southwest Texas. They worked in what is called *"la espiga,"* which means the sprig or tuft which grows on corn. The job entails going from corn stalk to corn stalk, breaking of the *"espiga"* from each and every plant. They also worked cleaning around the cotton plant. This involved taking a hoe and removing any sort of weed that might threaten the successful crop of cotton for that year.

TALES FROM THE TORTILLA CURTAIN

Role graduated from Eagle Pass High School in 1983. While attending the University of Texas at Austin, he encouraged Rick to come to the big city and begin a new life there. Also while in Austin, Role met Lewanda Lou Fields. They dated for about three years and eventually married on June 27, 1987. After graduating from UT, Role and Lewanda moved to Denton, Texas, where Role attained a Master's degree in Drama. Both Role and Lewanda went on to work on a Master's degree at Texas Woman's University. Lewanda graduated with a Master's degree in Theatre Directing. Role graduated with a Master's degree in English, with a Spanish minor. In the fall of 1990, Role and Lewanda moved to Lawrence, Kansas to pursue their Ph.D.'s at the University of Kansas. They each started in their respective fields--Role in English, Lewanda in Theater. However, because of financial complications. They each had to leave school to pursue full-time jobs. Role went on to serve as the Assistant Director of Minority Affairs at KU. On June 29, 1993, Role and Lewanda moved to Stillwater, Oklahoma, where Role was hired as the Hispanic and Vietnamese American Coordinator at Oklahoma State University. In April of 1997, they moved to Kearney, Nebraska, where Role assumed the position of Director of the office of Multicultural and International Student Services at the University of Nebraska at Kearney. Role went on to get a Master's degree in Bilingual Education / ESL while serving as Director of Student Life at

The University of Texas of the Permian Basin in Odessa in 2008.

As Role and Lewanda were doing their thing, Rick spent the next few years working in the Austin Independent School District as a teacher's aid. As time went by, Rick developed a great fascination with the concept of time travel. In researching the many theories on the subject, Rick came to understand how each theory might be worked out.

It must also be noted that on Thanksgiving night of 1993, Oscar, Role's best friend in Junior High School, was killed in a truck accident in Piedras Negras, Coahuila, Mexico. Each brother, having lost the childhood friend with whom they had shared so many experiences, then turned to the only other person who had been there for almost everything--each other.

This brings us to this point along the continuum. Just because this is how things have happened this time does not mean that they have always happened this way, or that they will continue in the fashion forever. If there is a moral to these stories, it is that it is never too late to take charge of your life and to make it a good one. Any tool, whether it be a time machine or the right frame of mind, has the potential to change your life.

THE LETTER

What is the fabric of time, and what is it ultimately made of? Is it a single continuum from which there is no escape? Is it a finely knit piece of interwoven possibilities? What will happen if a piece of the fabric is torn off or at least changed? Will the effects ripple throughout the fabric itself and ultimately change even the most remote corner of existence and time? To be and not to be, that is the infinite choice, and the ultimate question, that two brothers set out to discover and finally, at least for themselves, answer.

It all started when Rick and his brother, Role, were thinking about how it might be possible to travel through time. The idea of having to go faster than light seemed to pose a real problem, being that faster-than-light travel had not even been invented yet. One day the two brothers were out walking around in the woods behind Role's house when they came upon something that seemed to appear out of nowhere. It seemed to be made of some sort of aluminum-colored metal. They proceeded to examine it and discovered that it was indeed some sort of wedge-shaped vehicle.

Rick touched the side of the ship and the side door opened with a hiss. They both went inside. There were two prominent chairs at the front of the ship and four other chairs directly behind. Noticing what appeared to be an old and quite worn envelope, Rick motioned Role over to him.

"Hey, Role." he said. "Check this out."

"What is it?"

"I don't know. Looks like some sort of old and quite worn envelope. What do you suppose it has inside?"

"I don't know, Rick. Open it up and see."

At this Rick pulled open the seal and took out the letters and documents that were contained therein. The main document read as follows:

"Dear Rick and Role,

We are sending you this letter and this time machine as part of a self-fulfilling prophesy. We, your counterparts from the year 2050, have sent this machine back in time so that you will have the same opportunity we did to travel through time. If you do not take this chance, then the future as we know it will never exist. In essence, you have to do what we have already done so that the right circumstances will exist for the time machine to ever be created in the first place. When we were in your situation, we took the time machine to a great many places and came to fulfill our own destinies. Now, it is our turn to give this time machine up. It must happen this way because this is the way it has always happened. Any deviation from the way it is supposed to happen will mean certain disaster for our, and your, future.

But, alas! We cannot tell you about the adventures you are about to undertake! If we tell you which things you are to do and which things you are to avoid, we would in effect be changing the future.

A word of warning, however. If you decide to travel into the future DO NOT attempt to look us up. You may travel anywhere you like, but for our sakes, please do not try to find us in the future. The temptation to tell you things would be too great, and that information, as we have already stated, would be of great danger to the future of your very lives.

Now then, we must discuss some of the neat gadgets that come with this time machine. This first one, located in the cabinet on the right side of the ship, is called the personal hologram projector (PHP), and there are six of them, one for each of the passengers you will carry aboard this ship. What the PHP does is project an image which envelops the person wearing it. This is primarily for your protection as well as for the protection of those with whom you will come in contact during your travels. The device itself has a memory of some twenty-two quadrillion bits, so chances are that it already has the image of anyone you could possibly imagine. Even then, you can still add to the number of images that it can project. Being that we have already been through what you are about to undertake, chances are that the images you will have it project are already programmed into it. That is not to say, however, that you will necessarily make the same choices we did, for time as we all know, is not constant, and neither are the events which happen within it. This device also has a personal communicator built into it. All you have to do is press the gold button located at its center and you will be able to communicate with the ship or with another person wearing a PHP.

The next device, located in a cabinet at the right side of the ship, can at best be called a stun gun. If you are to travel through time, the last thing you want to do is to kill someone whose offspring might eventually have a direct bearing on your very existence. This device will produce unconsciousness at a range of about one-hundred feet. Yes, Role, it resembles a phaser from your favorite T.V. show, but this one cannot disintegrate anything, just knock it out for a while, giving you the necessary time to take whatever action you need.

The next cabinet, located at the center of the ship, contains currency from every one of the major time periods. If you need currency from a period that is not represented here, simply have the replicator give you the amount you need. There are those who would have ethical problems with this device being that what it does strongly resembles counterfeiting. But, the truth of the matter is that it creates the currency from the sub-atomic level up, so that, in effect, it is just as real and valid as what might be called the real thing.

The two large cabinets at the rear of the ship contain the fiber/protein matter which the food replicator uses to make any food you might desire. If this supply is ever used up, all you have to do is use the transforming device, also at the rear of the ship, to transform, say a ten pound rock, into the fiber/protein material, and then transform the fiber/protein material into the desired food. As you can see, as long as matter exists, you will be able to have food to feed yourselves.

By now you may be wondering about the power source of this vehicle. It basically runs on a matter/antimatter reaction, the chamber for which is located beneath, behind, and on top of the ship. The matter collecting unit is located at the bottom of the ship. It basically collects matter constantly, even when the ship is standing still, until the chamber is full. The antimatter collecting unit is located at the top of the ship. This unit collects antimatter only while the ship is traveling through space. Once the chamber is full, it, too, stops collecting. Both the matter and the antimatter are then fed into the reaction core located at the back of the ship. As you can see, you will have a never-ending supply of fuel with which to run the ship.

Note: You must constantly monitor the matter/antimatter injection system. It must always read at .0627. Adjust the gage when necessary.

As you probably remember from your favorite time-travel movie, you will need to be properly attired when you visit any historical period in which you do not want to use the PHP. In this event, the replicator located at the center of the left wall of the ship will produce the appropriate attire for you to wear. Your basic measurements at every age of your life, and those of the people you are likely to request costumes for have already been programmed into its memory. All you have to do is ask it for what you want.

The only limitation in the ship that we can think of is that it can only carry six people, yourselves and four others. The allowed weight for each person is a generous three-hundred pounds, so chances are that you will never have a problem as far as having too much body weight on board. Be aware, however, that too much weight of any kind will result in irreparable damage to the internal structure of the ship.

The guidance system of the ship is located at the front left position. It is not all that different from driving a car, except that the hover mode might be a little tricky at first. You may wish to practice, unseen by anyone of course, before you attempt to navigate in this mode. You must pull the steering wheel toward you if you want to ascend and away from you if you want to descend. For further instructions, please consult the *Time Machine Owner's Manual*.

The time destination keys are located in the

front right position. Essentially, you type in the exact time, down to the very millisecond, and the exact place you wish to visit. The ship must be traveling at a constant speed of 186,000 miles per second, yes, the speed of light, with structural integrity shields fully operational, for the time disruption to occur. For this reason, you must be in orbit around the earth before you engage the time travel sequence. Remember that the antimatter collectors will be constantly working, and space is the best place to collect this stuff.

In any event, that about covers what you really need to know about where everything is and how it works. Again, if you have any further questions, please consult the *Time Machine Owner's Manual* located under the seat of the right front position.

We guess that is all. You might want to hang on to this letter so that you can pass it on to the other Rick and Role who come after you. You dudes have fun. And, uh, don't do anything we wouldn't, or didn't, do.

signed,

Rick and Role

2050 A.D."

Rick folded up the letter and looked around the ship.

"Wow, Role! Check it out!"

"I guess we finally achieved time travel!"

Their adventures were about to begin.

265

THE FIRST TRIP

The sun was coming up slowly on Trinity Street. The red bricks on the outside of Meche's Store looked like they were painted in pastel colors. Meche, a seventy-year-old woman with rollers in her hair, went about the daily business of opening up her neighborhood store. The dogs barked somewhere in the neighborhood. Huevos rancheros and tortillas filled the air with their aroma. "Me calli de la nuve mas alta" played on the radio.

Somewhere over the North American Continent, Rick and Role made the jump along the space/time continuum and appeared on September 13, 1972 over Eagle Pass, Texas.

"Are we there yet, Role?", asked Rick, looking out the window at the blue and white globe beneath them.

"I don't know. The computer says that we have arrived at the year 1972. We are now headed for Eagle Pass, Texas."

"What do you remember about that year?"

"Well, If I remember correctly, I was in second grade. Miss Owens was my teacher. Wasn't that the year that your teacher brought you into my class and I ran up to you guys and showed you that thing that we, as a class, were working on?"

"Yeah! We walked in. You ran up and showed me something. I can't quite remember what it was, but it was some sort of art or something."

"I'm setting the coordinates for Graves Elementary School on Kelso Drive. According to this, we'll be there in about five minutes. Do you want to use the personal holograph projector or wear period costume?"

"I don't know, Role. What do you think?"

"Well, dude. I think we should just wear period costume. You know, bell bottoms, slick shirts, thick belts. What do you remember wearing, Rick?"

"Something along the lines of *The Brady Bunch*."

They went over to the costume replicator and set it to replicate clothing from the early part of the 1970's. After a few seconds, the clothes appeared. Once dressed, they sat at the controls again.

"There's Eagle Pass right there!"

Suddenly a red light went off and an alarm sounded.

"Warning! We are visible to the naked eye. Ship-wide holograph shield must be initiated! Holograph shield must be initiated!"

"Engage holograph shield!" Role shouted.

"Holograph shield activated."

TALES FROM THE TORTILLA CURTAIN

The ship came to rest on the open field behind Graves Elementary School. A few short mesquite trees were crushed under the weight of the ship.

"Look, dude! There's Graves Elementary. Before it was remodeled in the mid-seventies."

Role was getting some currency out of the case in which it was contained.

"How much money do you think we'll need, Rick?"

"Let me have about a hundred bucks in ones, fives, tens, and twenties."

"I think I'll take about a hundred bucks too."

They opened the hatch door and proceeded slowly out of the ship. The hot September air was the first thing that hit their faces. Next came all the smells that they had long since forgotten. The smell of the dry southwest Texas air came next. And the memories that came with those smells! The great beauty of it all was that here they were, about to observe some of these memories all over again.

In the distance, Rick saw a group of kids playing and carrying on, like kids always do. As he approached, he saw a familiar face. The one that had always stared back at him through all those school pictures. The face that had so long ago left him from the other side of the mirror. There, playing with his friend Sammy was the younger version of Rick, Ricky as he was called then.

At first, all Rick could do was stand there in awe. What could he do? What could he say? If he were to say anything, would that change history?

And what about Sammy? Could he walk up and warn him about the motorcycle accident that would end his life?

"Rick, are you okay?" asked Role quietly.

"Yeah. I just didn't expect it to be this way."

"What did you expect?"

"I don't know. I expected to see what I remember, I guess. And I don't remember this particular moment in my life."

At this, some bully, whose name has been forgotten, came up and started to pick on young Ricky. This guy, who always seemed to emanate a not-exactly-clean aroma, was to become known as The Guy That Stinks. So, The Guy That Stinks came up to Ricky and started picking on him for no apparent reason. Ricky, not knowing what to do, just started to cry. The bell rang and the rest of the kids ran inside. Little Role came up and asked what had happened.

"Can you tell I've been crying?", asked Ricky, through bloodshot and watery eyes.

"No.", said Little Role as they both went inside the school.

"Why, that . . .", started Rick in a bit of anger.

"Rick, this incident happened a long time ago."

It is this type of anger, however, that follows us around for the rest of our lives. For these are the formative years, and whatever experiences we have do dictate the outcome of what we do later in life. His experience let Rick come to this realization.

"I know." he said, "But I still hate that dude."

"Where to first?", asked Role, trying to break the tension.

"I'm not sure I'm ready to deal with the way things are over at the Senior Moreno's apartment where we lived at this time."

"Let's go over to Meche's Store", said Role. "It's been so long since I've seen her. She did pass away in 1979."

They walked down Ferry Street, made a right turn onto Trinity Street, and walked the long block to the corner where Meche's Store was. They opened the wire screened door and walked in. And there she was. The short, somewhat heavily built woman, advanced in years, wearing rollers in her hair. The *chanklas* on her feet complimented the colors on her dress.

"Buenos dias.", said Role, looking in vain for some sort of recognition in the face of the of woman.

"Buenas, buenas.", she said, and resumed her work.

Here was the lady with whom Role had shared a special relationship as a child. How he had been bothered by the fact that he had shoveled dirt upon the very coffin of this woman, when he worked as a caretaker at the Eagle Pass Cemetery in the summer of 1979. But here she was, alive and well at this point along the continuum of space and time. Rick broke Role's silence by asking him what he wanted to drink.

"Oh, a Coke's fine. A real Coke Classic."

Rick walked over to the red steel Coca Cola cooler, pulled out two Cokes from the rack inside, and popped the tops off on the bottle opener on the right hand side of the cooler and walked over to Role. They both walked up to the counter.

"Cuanto es?", asked Role.

"Treinta centavos", said Meche who for a moment at least seemed to sense something very familiar in the eyes of the man before her.

She took the dollar bill and gave Role back the change.

"Gracias", she said.

"A usted." said Role.

Rick and Role stood there drinking their sodas, finished, and left the store.

"What a trip! The funny thing is that she seemed to recognize me."

"I don't know, Role. That's seems impossible. Yes, we do carry some of the same physical traits throughout our lives, but I don't know about her actually recognizing you. She did look at you kind of weird, though."

"I tell you what. Let's go down Ferry Street, make a left on Medina, and go down Main Street. It might be pretty cool to go downtown and see the old Aztec Theater the way it used to be."

"Sure. Let's go."

Before too long, Rick and Role found themselves standing in front of the Aztec Theater. It looked the way Rick and Role had always remembered it in their youth. The neon arrows were all still working in their perpetual motion. The all-too-familiar smell of popcorn emanated from inside the movie house.

"So, do you want to go in, Rick?"

"Yeah, man, let's check it out!"

They both paid their way into the theater and soon found themselves standing at the refreshment counter.

"Let me have a 45 cent bag of popcorn, a hot dog, and a coke.", Role told one of the two old ladies behind the counter.

"Make that two of the same." Rick said.

They paid the other lady and proceeded to the upstairs balcony of the theatre.

"Wait, dude." Role said, "I need to get some Junior Mints from the machine." He put in the fifteen cents for his candy, pulled the handle, heard the box of candy drop, and took it.

They walked up the dark and musty smelling steps. The smell itself was always a mix of cigarette smoke, popcorn, and sweat, for it was always hot in Eagle Pass.

Just as they were about to sit down at their seats, there was a loud noise from the downstairs area. The doors flew open and eight men ran in, all dressed in the green uniforms of the Border Patrol.

"What the hell is that, Rick?"

"I don't know, dude, but it looks like a raid on the Aztec."

"So what are we going to do?"

"Chill, man. All you have to do is speak

English. They'll leave you alone if you just speak English."

One of the Border Patrol men, a man named Beauley, came upstairs. He saw Rick and Role and came over to them. This guy looked like he had a little too much bad attitude, which showed in the way he walked.

"American citizens?" he said.

"No, dude, we're from the planet Vulcan. My name is Spock and this here's Kirk!" said Role, who had always been a *Star Trek* fan.

"Actually, we are American citizens." Rick said, trying to prevent a situation that might arise from Role's sarcastic remark.

"You fellers got any sort of identification?" the Beauley asked.

At this, Rick and Role looked at each other, remembering that they had failed to replicate some sort of identification. Their own identification, from their own time, was back in the time machine.

"I apologize for my sense of humor" said Role, "I really meant no harm."

"We'll just see about that. Let's see your identification."

"We left it at home, but if you wait here, we can easily go there and get it." said Rick.

"You two look like you're hiding something. You gonna have to come with me."

What were Rick and Role to do now? They had no place to go at this time. If they were to tell this man that they were time travelers, they would seem even sillier than the science-fiction movie that was on the screen. The only thing that they could do was to find some way to escape from the Aztec Theater and find their way back to the time machine and leave this time. But how could they do it?

"The guy running the film projector is also with us. Can we ask him to come along?" Rick said.

Beauley walked up the steps which led to the projection booth and knocked. When no one answered, he opened the door. At this Rick pushed the guy in and closed the door behind him. He then took a broom handle that was leaning against the wall and jammed it against the door handle.

"Let's go, dude!" Rick shouted.

They were about to down the stairs when they heard two other patrolmen coming up the stairs.

Role noticed that a small window was open at the back wall of the theater. It opened out over the Aztec Theater sign, but it was their only hope of escape.

"Up there!"

They both ran and squeezed through the small window. Once outside, they walked along the ledge and jumped onto a fire escape ladder that was beside the building and climbed down. As they did this, they could hear Beauley screaming and hollering from the projection booth.

Once on the street, Rick and Role made a run for it. Because there was so much confusion in the raid of the theater itself, they managed to make it as far as the town library. They walked in and sat down on one of the leather-upholstered sofas.

"What do we do now?" asked Role.

"We're going to have to be a lot more careful. This reality is just as dangerous as the one we left."

"It might be a good idea to get back to the time machine and get out of here. That guy knows what we look like, and he'll notice that we're not in with the group that is taken to the detention center."

"We should probably get back to Graves Elementary by sticking to the back streets." Role whispered, because they were beginning to gather attention.

They both got up and made their way to the glass double doors at the back entrance of the library. Just as they were about to open them, the man in the green uniform jumped in their path, swung open the door, and pulled out his pistol.

"I knew you two would be around here. What's the matter. You lost? The river is in the other direction!" Beauley said, smiling a smile which revealed a set of teeth were decaying from a constant use of chewing tobacco.

The drive to the border patrol station was not exactly a pleasant one. The back of the pickup truck was filled with illegals who had also been caught in the raid on the Aztec Theater. The air was filled with the body odor of the ten men who were crammed into such a small confined space.

Each of the detainees was pushed into a small holding cell to await the deportation procedure. Rick and Role sat in one of the steel bunks and wondered how they would ever get out of this one. The great irony was that this was but their first trip in the time machine. Now their carelessness might cost them dearly.

"Wait a minute." said Role. "If we were able to come back from the future to give ourselves the time machine, we surely get out of this somehow. All it takes is figuring out what we have that we can use to our advantage."

"Really. What is the main reason we are being held? We may be Hispanic, but we certainly don't sound like the rest of the men in this cell."

"But, the only reason we are being held is that we don't have any sort of identification. How can we prove that we are American citizens?" asked Role.

At this point, one of the border patrol men came into the room in which the cell was located. He stood at the other side of the bars and called out to Rick and Role.

"You two, please walk this way." he said.

"Are we going to be deported to Mexico?" asked Rick.

"No," the man said coldly, "the only reason you were held was that you did not have any identification. Your father and your uncle just arrived and they brought it for you. You two are obviously American citizens, so you are free to go. We are sorry for any inconvenience."

"Father and uncle. That's impossible!" said Role.

They were escorted to the main desk and handed their wallets.

"Positive identification." the patrolman said.

Rick and Role walked out into the Texas air wondering just who could have saved them from their trouble, when they saw two men and a brown dog getting into an old pickup truck. The two men looked at them and smiled.

"Who is that?"

"Could it be . . . us?" asked Role.

At this, the two old men simply disappeared.

"The hologram projector! That wasn't any pickup truck at all. That was the time machine they just got into!" exclaimed Rick.

"I wonder just how many times we are going to save ourselves in our travels."

"I don't know, dude, but let's get away from this station as soon as possible."

They walked across the street and stood at the entrance of *El Cenizo Drive-In*. This was an old drive-in movie theater that was eventually torn down to make room for a shopping center.

"We're close enough, Rick. Do you want to do it?"

"What? Go see where we used to live?"

"Yes."

They walked over to Pecos Street and made their way over to *el Senior Moreno's* apartments. They walked down the long driveway and stared at the house where they had spent a few years of their youth.

And there she was, still looking young and carrying on in her household duties--Mom. She was visible through the main window in the living room of the house. As they stood there, a brown dog came up and sniffed at their ankles. Rick and Role looked at each other and then at the dog.

"Rusty!" they shouted.

Here was the dog that they had had when they were children. But here he was still very much alive and wagging its tail in recognition.

"Do you suppose he recognizes us?"

"I don't know, Role. But I don't remember him being this friendly."

"How are you, boy!" said Role, tenderly petting the dog.

"It's too bad that he goes on to get the mange and Mom has Dad take him out beyond the city limits and leave him there.", said Rick, remembering the bitter disappointment he had felt then.

"Do you suppose that we can jump ahead in time to when that happens and rescue him?" asked Role.

"How? I don't remember the exact date when it happens."

"I tell you what. Let's go back to the time machine and check the computer for significant dates in our lives. It might be in there." said Rick. At this, they left their childhood friend behind and walked over to Graves Elementary School.

It was a little after three in the afternoon. The children had just been let out. They saw Ricky and Sammy walking together. The Guy That Stinks walked up and started picking on the two kids. Rick walked over and grabbed the bully by his shirt.

"¡Dejalos!" he said.

The Guy That Stinks started crying and begging to be put down. Once on his feet, he ran away down Kelso Drive.

"He won't bother you anymore." Rick told his younger self.

Sammy just stood there laughing.

"Baighng!" Rick said, giving himself the old and familiar greeting that only he and Sammy had ever known.

"Are you sure you should have said that? You and Sammy didn't use that word to greet each other until you were in junior high school." said Role.

"I always wondered who it was that saved me from the Guy That Stinks that day. I guess now I know."

They made their way to the open field behind Graves Elementary and found the ship there, still cloaked. Once inside, they accessed the personal history computer and asked for the precise date when Rusty was taken out to be left beyond the city limits.

"September 19, 1973, 3:30 p.m." it said.

"Computer," Role said, "set the destination time and place as September 19, 1973, 3:30 p.m., Eagle Pass Texas and prepare to engage."

"Acknowledged."

Rick sat in the pilot's chair at the front of the ship and Role sat in the chair of co-pilot. Around fifty feet from the ship, they saw Beauley skulking around the empty lot behind Graves. He was apparently still out looking for illegals.

"Are you thinking what I'm thinking" asked Rick.

"You bet." said Role.

As they were leaving, the compressed air coming from the hover units surprised the same overzealous, tobacco-chewing patrolman who had been so abusive earlier and knocked him on his butt.

"Engage ship-wide hologram projector to emit the image of a pterodactyl with the head of a pig. Let's give him a taste of *el pajaro gigante*," Role said.

"The Giant Bird legend? But that doesn't happen for a few more years, Role."

"Gotta start somewhere!"

Old Beauley looked up and saw the great image of the bird with the face of a pig and cried out in terror. He ran, slid face-first into an *arroyo*, and passed out.

"Well, that takes care of him."

They piloted the ship up into the blue sky high over Eagle Pass and prepared to engage the time travel sequence. Soon, they were surrounded by the darkness of space.

"Computer, engage time traveling procedure." Role said.

In a brilliant flash of light they accelerated to light speed and made the jump.

"Time and place?"

"Time: September 19, 1973, 3:30 p.m. Place: North American Continent." the computer answered.

"Let's go get Rusty and get out of here. I can't wait to get back to our own time." said Rick.

They came down to Eagle Pass and flew the ship along the Del Rio highway. Far below them, they saw an old beige Ford truck.

"There they are!"

They saw the truck stop, their dad get out and take the dog out of the truck. They saw how he petted the dog gently and regrettably got back inside the truck. He sat there for a minute or two as the dog looked at him confusedly. He turned on the truck and left.

Rick and Role set the ship down around ten feet from where Rusty was and called out to him.

"Rusty! Come here, boy!"

The dog wagged its tail in recognition and came running.

"We'll give you a bath and cure you of your mange when we get you home, boy!"

Rick said.

"We need to strap him down. He doesn't need to be running around the ship." said Role.

They strapped him to the passenger's seat behind the co-pilot's chair as Rusty patiently sat there and let them do it.

"Let's go home, Rick" Role said when they finished.

Before too long, they were once again flying over the North American Continent.

"Prepare for the jump!" Role said.

In the brilliant flash of light that was to become an all too familiar sight in their later adventures, Rick and Role were once again back in their own time.

"I guess we made it. Computer, are we back in our own time?

"Affirmative. This is the time from which this voyage was originally started."

"We must learn to be more careful in the future." Role said. "This time we did things that could have had some serious repercussions on future incidents."

"The next time we do this, we'll have to plan the entire thing very carefully. We must be prepared for any emergency that comes up."

In any event, this was the first trip that Rick and Role took in the time machine. It was to be the first of the many great adventures that they would take in their search for moments in time which held the answers to timeless questions.

PREVENTION

Rick and Role were doing some minor adjustments on the Cesar Chavez, for that was what they had named the ship. Role even went so far as to cut out a picture of the man himself from an old United Farm Workers poster and hang it from the dashboard. A small red flag with the black eagle inside the white circle could be seen to the left of the picture.

According to the manual, the matter/antimatter injection unit had to be monitored regularly, or else the ship would quite simply run out of fuel. The injection matrix would not run consistently, and the ship would essentially fail to function.

"It says here that the way to calibrate the injection system is to adjust the electronic gage to read .0627." said Role.

".0625 . . . 0626 . . . 0627." Rick called out, adjusting the gage as he went.

"All of the other stuff seems to be running perfectly.

Computer, begin a level Alpha diagnostic systems check."

"Working."

After a few moments, the computer called out, "All systems working within acceptable parameters. Please check the . . . CODE 9." The computer interrupted itself.

"What?"

"CODE 9."

"Explain what this means." Rick said into the computer.

"CODE 9 . . . historical adjustment necessary. Consult main computer for more information."

"Bring the main computer on-line" Rick said.

"Main computer. May I help you?"

"Explain the CODE 9 order."

The computer began, "A historical adjustment is necessary. There is a specific moment in time which must be adjusted in order for the universe and the reality which we know to continue."

"What historical adjustment?" Role asked.

"On June 11, 1962 Rick will be killed by an out of control delivery truck. You two must go back to that point in time and keep that incident from happening."

"Why must we go back and keep it from happening? If it didn't happen in the first place, why do we have to go back and keep it from happening now?" asked Rick.

"The reason it didn't happen in the first place is that you two went back and kept it from happening.

TALES FROM THE TORTILLA CURTAIN

Your other selves were the ones who kept the incident from happening the first time when you experienced the incident as children. Now the time has come for you two to go back as adults and keep the incident from happening. In essence, you must go back there and save Rick's life, otherwise, everything we know about him will never come to be. For all we know, this whole project might never exist, and the whole cycle in which we exist will be broken."

"Give me the exact time and place that this incident happens." said Role.

"April 11, 1965. 2:36 p.m. Theba, Arizona."

"Relay that information to the navigation computer." Rick said.

"Rick, what do you remember about that day? I know you were

a little kid, but surely you remember where you were or what you were doing."

"I was supposed to go fishing with my uncle Pedro that day. At least he told that was what we were going to do. He gathered his fishing gear and was all ready to cross the street to the canal which ran very close to where we used to live. I remember crossing the street with only one thing on my mind--catching some fish. I didn't see the delivery truck which came speeding down the road. I remember hearing the screeching of the tires and passing out. When I came to I was in a hospital bed. Mom told me that the truck never really touched me, but that I passed out from the shock of seeing that huge vehicle. The guy paid for every imaginable test to make sure that I was all right. I remember Mom always telling me about it when I was growing up."

"So there you have it. We have to go back there and keep you from getting killed. Do you remember what the man looked like?" asked Role.

"Barely. Computer, access the holographic image of the driver of the truck in the April 11, 1965 incident."

The computer remained silent and then projected the image of the man whom Rick had seen so many years ago.

"Just as I thought. Being that we keep giving this machine to ourselves at the end of every cycle, the computers are all already programmed with the information that we need to fulfill our missions to the past. The pairs of Ricks and Role change, but the time machine and all the information that it carries remain constant. You get it?" asked Rick.

"Being that this computer already knows what we have done during the previous cycles, the system already knows what we need and when we need it. The computer will always be one step ahead of us," Role said.

"One or fifty. It's all the same."

"So we are merely pawns in the cycle? Can we change anything? In trying to change something, are we merely doing what the previous pair of ourselves did?" asked Role.

"Negative." replied the computer. "The element of chance is always there. Just because the same thing has been done for a googol amount of times does not mean it will be repeated for a googol and one. The ultimate choice in what happens is yours."

They piloted the ship out of the garage where it was stored and headed for the great open space of the stratosphere.

"Begin the time traveling procedure and let me know when we are ready to make the jump." Rick said as he adjusted his place at the pilot's chair.

"Ready."

"Engage."

Before too long they found themselves hovering over the state of Arizona. The computer guided them over to where the incident was to happen. In two hours Rick's fate would be saved or sealed.

"Can you lock in on the whereabouts of the driver of the truck?"

"Affirmative."

"Where is he now?"

"He is having the brakes on his truck fixed at Chato's Garage. 257 Kathleen. He will be there for the next twenty minutes. It is imperative that you use the holograph projector and replace him as the driver of the truck."

"What'll we do with him? Walk up and ask if we can kindly borrow his truck?" asked Role.

"Use the hand weapon located in the compartment at the rear of the ship. Remember that it can be set on stun only. This man must be allowed to make his contribution to the world. His unborn offspring goes on to pioneer the work on time traveling."

Role reached for the hand weapon and held it in his hand. He then strapped on a personal holograph projector and joined Rick, who was already wearing his and waiting for him outside the ship.

"Engage the ship-wide hologram projector and secure the ship." Rick said.

"Ship secured" the computer responded through the personal communicator device within the hologram projector.

They each set the projector to emit the image of the clothing of the time.

"Okay, let's find this guy." Role said as they walked into town. As they approached the town, Role set his hologram projector for invisibility and disappeared.

Senior Hernandez was drinking a Coca-Cola and eating from a bag of peanuts as he leaned on the wall of the garage. He was a good man, and had always gone out of his way to help the migrant workers who were less fortunate.

Rick walked up to him and greeted him with the usual Spanish salutation.

"Buenos días." Rick said.

"Buenas."

"Ya mero?" Rick asked, wondering when the truck would be finished.

"Sí." Hernandez said. *"Ya esta lista."*

Hearing that the truck was ready, Role approached the man from behind and stunned him. Keeping the man within his own holographic field, Role managed to make Senior

Hernandez disappear just as the attendant came out of the station.

"Señor Hernandez. ¿Donde esta?" he asked, wondering where the man was.

"Aqui." Rick said from around the corner of he building. He appeared under the guise of Senior Hernandez.

"¿Cuanto?" he asked.

"Son siete dolares."

Rick pulled out the period money and handed him the seven dollars.

"Gracias." he said.

"A usted." the attendant responded.

They loaded the real Senior Hernandez into the back of the delivery truck and drove toward the place where Rick had lived as a child. There were only a few minutes left before the incident was to happen.

He turned left from Rosen Road onto Kathleen. He drove quickly, trying to remember the exact house that he had lived in.

"It's got to be here some place." he said. "I was so young."

"Eight minutes before the incident." Role said.

"Oh, man!" Rick shouted. "Look! We're on south Kathleen. The address we need is on the other end of this street. How can we get there in eight minutes?!"

"Speed it up!"

"I'm going as fast as I can!" Rick said as he made a very quick u-turn.

Before too long, they were in the right neighborhood. The houses went by in a quick blur.

"Where is he? Where is he?" Rick said.

"Watch it! There he is!!" Role shouted pointing to the child in the middle of the street.

No matter how much Rick tried to stop the truck, it remained out of control. In a flash it was over. The bloodied body of the child lay a few steps from the front hood of the truck.

"Oh, my God! What have I done?!" Rick said.

The mother of the child came running and screaming from inside the house. She held the body of the child in her arms.

"¡Mi hijo! ¡Mi hijito!" she cried.

"Role! Help me! Something's happening to me! Help me, Role!"

Role reached out to Rick but he was gone. The brother Role had always known was no more. From behind him, Role heard a voice--new, yet familiar.

"Role, what can we do about this?" the man asked.

"Who are you?" Role asked as he approached this man whose features were familiar also, but whom he had never met.

"Me? I'm Edward, dude! Are you okay?" said Role's brother whom Role had always known had died only a few hours after birth. Apparently, the future had already been changed. For an instant, Rick appeared back where Edward had been.

"Role, what's happening?"

"Rick, we have seriously affected the future.

The space/time continuum is trying to correct itself. Just now I saw, . . .", but before he could finish, Edward appeared.

" . . .Edward."

Rick appeared for another instant, then disappeared. Edward sat where Rick had been.

"Edward? But how can it be you? You. You're . . ."

"What? Listen, we have to help Mom get our brother Richard to the hospital. That is the reason we came on this trip. We can't simply sit around and look lost. We have to help Mom!"

"But, . . ." Role cut his sentence in mid-speech. He realized that the only way the repair the future was to go back in time to when he and Rick made the wrong turn on Kathleen and ended up on the wrong side of town.

"I have to get back to the ship." He told Edward. For a moment, he stared at his other brother and wondered if there would ever be a way for he and Rick to save him.

"You stay here with Mom. Do what you can. I'll be right back. There is something in the ship that will save Rick's life." Role said.

"And it will cost you yours." he thought to himself.

He started running toward the place where they had left the ship. When he got there, he jumped into the pilot's chair and maneuvered the ship into a high orbit over North America. When he made the jump to one hour earlier, he came down and landed the ship a block away from where it had been before. He secured the ship and ran toward the service station where he knew Rick and Role would be at this time.

And there they were. Along this timeline, however, Edward and Role were the ones approaching the service station where Senior Hernandez was drinking his coke and eating his peanuts. Role turned on his holograph projector to project the image of an old man. He reached Edward and Role.

"Remember that you must get to Kathleen. Not South Kathleen. You must make a right turn not a left one. The future of your brother depends on it." he said.

"Are you . . . ?" Edward asked.

"Yes." Role responded.

He walked away and let them carry on in their mission. Would this fix the mistake that had happened earlier? There was only one way to find out. He would have to jump ahead into time one hour. To the exact time he had left the scene of the accident and see if Rick's life had been spared.

After making the jump and landing the ship right where it had been before, Role ran over to the scene of the accident. When he got there, there was a man with his back to Role and holding a child. When the man turned around it was Rick, and the child was in his arms, alive and well. Edward was nowhere to be found. For once again, he had died as a child. Evidently, Edward had made the right turn along Kathleen and caused Rick's life to be saved.

The tragedy was that Edward in effect sealed his own fate in saving Rick's life.

On the journey back to their own time, Role remained very quiet. Rick sat in the pilot's chair.

"Why are you so quiet, Role."

"Do you know what happened down there?"

"What do you mean?"

"I mean we failed the first time we tried to save your life. For a brief moment in time Edward was alive in this time. When you died as a child, he was allowed to live. When I went back and corrected the continuum, he died once again."

For the rest of the journey, the two brothers who once were three sat there in silence.

FANTASTIC CATALOG

(The following entry is taken from the personal logs of Rolando J. Diaz aboard the Time Vehicle Cesar Chavez. Time along the continuum: June 27, 1992.)

My wife, Lewanda, and I always get rather peculiar catalogs in the mail. Some advertise housewares, others advertise appliances and electronics, while still others try to sell sleepwear and lingerie. Well, today I am checking the mail, as I am want to do every day at approximately one o'clock in the afternoon. I put the key into the mailbox lock, and there it is. A catalog addressed to Role Diaz. I bring it home and set it upon the coffee table.

I briefly look through the catalog because my eyes are still tired from another late night of grading papers and preparing for class. Some of the things this catalog contains are, to say the least, fantastic. Page one contains the Personal Library Book Locator. According to the description, it interfaces

297

with a library's main system, by remote, and instantly tells you exactly which books are still on the shelves. If that is not enough, this gadget comes with a sensor which tells you exactly where the book is on the shelves and how to get there. If the book is located on the third floor of the library, the unit will tell you which elevator to take to the third floor, which way to turn once you get off the elevator, and which shelf, lower, middle, or upper, that the book is on.

If you need to find the bathroom, the unit will also tell you which floors the bathrooms are on and how to get there. Amazing invention, but not all that improbable, considering that it merely incorporates what already exists.

There is another neat invention advertised on the next page. It is an automatic pilot for your car. According to the ad, it uses fuzzy logic to see and recognize the roadways which are programmed into it. It can sense other cars if they come too close. If your car begins to run out of gas, and you are asleep at the wheel, the unit's voice will gently wake and ask you to direct the car to the nearest gas station, and proceed to show you the nearest, quickest way to get there.

There is also a unit which monitors the speed at which your car travels. It takes cruise control a step further. It, too, uses fuzzy logic in that it monitors road signs and is able to recognize and interpret speed limit signs. So, if you happen to be in, shall we say, Oklahoma City at around three in the morning and you happen to notice a plethora of police cars pulling people over for speeding, you might want to engage your Speed Monitor to be sure that you are not pulled over by an over-anxious police person.

Interesting device.

What's this? A hoverboard recreation area. You get twenty square feet of highly magnetized floor mat and a board which has been equipped with two magnets of the opposite polarity from the mat. Hmmm. Fun for the whole family. I wonder how they ever overcame the dangers of magnetic fields on the human body.

Here's something neat. Television monitors which can be strapped to the backs of car seats. These monitors are hooked up to a main video cassette recorder and player which serves as the main unit which emits the television signal. This would be great for long trips. The Back Seat Theatre comes with the VCR and two television monitors. Others monitors can be purchased separately. Asterisk--these monitors can also be linked to video game units.

The more advanced model, also the more expensive one, comes with a built-in video disk player. This one can operate independently from all the rest. Of course, all of the units come with their own sets of ear phones.

That would make a nice stocking stuffer.

Here's something for the health conscious. A workout gym which lets you lose weight and firm and develop your muscles while you engage on a mind vacation. Three times a week you attach the electrodes to your major muscle groups for isometric exercise while you go off on a virtual reality trip.

Hmmm. That wouldn't be too bad.

I close the catalog. I rub my tired eyes and look at the catalog's cover. The price of the catalog is seventy-five dollars. It is the Spring 2019 Catalog for Dayfields Inc. There must be some mistake. This is the year 1992. How is it that this has been mailed to us? I put the magazine on the coffee table and go into the kitchen to make a pot of coffee.

There is a strange blue light from the living room. I turn the corner to see an old man dressed in a very futuristic mail man's outfit.

"Sorry," he says, "we usually run a little late with the mail. But sometimes we run a little bit early. Right person" he says with a smile, "Wrong year. Have a good day." He opens the front door and is gone. I run after him, but only witness the dimming sparkle of the blue light.

I'll probably place an order for some of the things in that catalog, but I'll have to wait twenty-seven years for delivery.

OUR KORTANIAN FRIEND

During one of our travels, Rick and I met a strange looking fellow who related this story to us. It seems that his people can only tell stories in the present tense, because to them, it all happens at the same time. They have no past, present, or future. All they have is the sense of now, where everything is experienced simultaneously.

Rick and I sat there in that futuristic bar as this creature re-enacted the adventure he had experienced in his youth, way before humans and Kortanians ever developed any sort of diplomatic relations.

He went into a sort of trance, as Kortanians are apt to do, and related his story as follows:

"The forward propulsion units are no longer working. The last attack on the ship has finally taken its toll. There are only a few minutes left before the total destruction of the main hull. The only chance I have left is to leave the ship via the escape pod which I have just entered.

The onboard computer continues its final countdown.

In theory, the computer onboard this escape pod should be able to handle the sum of the knowledge of the ship's computer. I must download the ship computer's memory to this one, and hurry.

A few seconds pass and the all clear sign comes up on the screen. The soul of the main ship has now been passed to this one.

I am free of the main ship. As I move away from it, I can see the devastation that the attack of the humans has had on the ship.

"We come in peace." we told them.

But they never extended their hand to us. How foolish we were to actually believe humans to be trustworthy. The other members of the galactic family warned us about trying to make first contact with humans. They warned us that humans are very vicious and ruthless people. They will kill one another for something as simple as a natural resource. They cannot ever be trusted.

Oh, computer. You are my only companion now. This pod is said to hold enough provisions for at least five lifetimes. So here I am. All of infinity at my disposal. Will I ever reach my home world of Kortana? The computer tells me that we have enough fuel to get there, but the trip will take so many years. We can only travel at three times the speed of light.

But there is little we can do. Computer, are you on-line?

Yes I am. How can I help you?

You are to be my one companion as we travel toward home. What do you think of that?

I rather like the idea. I noticed that you were paying too much attention to your Kortanian companions. I may be a computer, but I have feelings too. Will you sing to me?

Me? Sing? What kind of a request is that for a computer to make?

A very reasonable one. I happen to know that you have a very nice tenor voice which you only use while in the shower.

Have you spied on me before?

Only when my sensors detect your voice.

Can you tell me how long it will take to make this voyage to Kortana?

The voyage will take approximately one hundred and fifty six years. You know that we cannot travel at the same speed as the main ship.

Will I survive the trip?

I am here to keep you company.

This is such a confined space. How can I possibly stay here for such a long time?

Do you see that headset to your right?

Yes.

Put it on.

What is it?

Trust me. Put it on.

Okay. There.

Are you ready to take a little trip?

Yes.

Here we go.

What's happening? How did we get here? Look at the purple sky. The wide open space. The orange vegetation. I have only read about places like this.

This unit will allow us to travel to any place you could ever dream of. This is just a sampling I knew you would be familiar with. I am also able to manifest myself into any form you wish. Do you find this appealing?

My, you are beautiful. Your blue hair and silver skin certainly flatter you. Can I hold you and put your lips to mine? Yes.

This will certainly make the trip home much more enjoyable.

Will you have some wine? Riterian wine. Almost three centuries old.

Yes.

Thank you. It's delicious. But wait a minute. Something's wrong.

What is it?

I taste this but it has no substance. Can you correct it?

I can stimulate your motor sensory responses. I can also feed you intravenously. You will be able to stay in this reality while your body is enclosed in that escape pod on its voyage home. Sleep now. And let me take care of the rest. Sleep.

I wake up. The smell of the morning coffee stirs me from my slumber. Meg sleeps beside me. How I have loved you all these years. There is nothing I would not do for her. She is the one who gives my life meaning and direction.

The morning sun comes in through the bedroom window. It gives everything in this room a golden glow. My high school diploma. Amazing achievement that was. A few degrees later and here I am, pilot in the space program.

I make my way to the first floor of the house. Down the stairs. Turn to the left and there's the kitchen. The coffee's done. Probably has been for the last twenty minutes. I just love automatic things.

I pick up the morning newspaper. Says here that a new life form has made first contact with the planet earth. How many newspapers do they think they will sell with a headline like this? I never thought the *Times* would stoop to printing something this idiotic.

We told them that this headline would only serve to start mass hysteria. People have already been reported jumping off buildings and committing mass suicide because they feel the end of the world is at hand.

Bastards. The media are the ones who are at fault here, not us. We have already made contact and we have already decided that contact is not wanted. These off-worlders have no place among the human races of the earth. The last thing we need is another race to come in and compete with us for the few menial jobs that are left.

They claim to have superior power and new

technological advances. They don't look that new or superior to me. For all we know, they are just little green men from Mars. Ha, ha. Joke.

No, but seriously, there can be no contact with other worlds. Our scientists have proven that there is no such thing as life on other planets. Why do these creatures dare to prove the very fabric of our culture wrong? Don't they realize that to admit to life on other planets would be to admit that man is not superior in the universe? No, that is not possible.

I take a cup of coffee to my wife. How I love her so. She stirs. I kiss her. She opens her eyes and looks at me the way she did on our wedding night.

Are you happy?

Yes, I am.

Is this all that you have ever wanted?

Yes.

I kiss her. She kisses back. We roll around the bed in each other's arms.

Late in the afternoon I get a phone call. It's my commanding officer. He tells me that the negotiations between earth and the Kortanians have taken a turn for the worst. We are but a few days from all out war against these creatures.

I hang up and turn to my wife.

You do this for me?

I do this for the good of all people.

Why?

Our way of life must be maintained. There can be no other race which may dominate man. We must be the superior beings in the universe.

You will destroy them then?

Yes. If I have to.

They came in peace. Why must you kill them to prove that we are peaceful, too?

There is peace in a balance of power. If we don't attack them, they will only enslave our people with their technology.

Is that what we would do?

Yes.

Is this what it is like to be human?

Yes.

Killing to show that killing is wrong?

These aliens must know that humans are not to be trifled with.

I see my child enter from the upstairs. She looks at me innocently.

Are you going away, Daddy?

Yes, Una, I am.

Why?

There is something that your daddy has to do to make your life better.

Mommy says that you are going to kill people. Is that true?

These things are not people. They come from a far away place. They want to make life bad for people here on earth. You don't want that do you?

How can we know that life will be bad, Daddy? Have they told you? No.

Why must you kill them?

Because that is the way things have always

been, Una.

Can they change?

If I were going up I would not kill them. I would talk to them to see what they want.

Perhaps, but it will take more than a little girl's wishes to stop this encounter with the Kortanians.

Days later I think about what my child has said. Perhaps there is some truth there. I receive my orders. The days that have passed have only served to strengthen the earth's forces against the Kortanians. We are sending up one ship to attack the Kortanian mothership. This is all that we have been able to come up with in such a short time. I can only hope that the weapons we have jury-rigged will be any sort of match for them.

The earth's gravity pulls against my flesh. I feel every inch of my body strained under the great thrust of the ship.

Orbit. And there it is. They do not threaten us with weapons. They threaten us with new ideas and that is bad enough. I must save the human race from such things. It must never know that life exists on other planets. The fools who published that report in the newspaper will soon be discounted as loons and idiots. Just like all of those who have reportedly seen Elvis still alive even to this day.

They will not fire on this ship. They have said so many times over. They will sit there and be destroyed if that proves that they mean no harm. Well, we will take them up on that offer.

Fire, you bastards! I can only sit here so long!

They do nothing.

I fire a nuclear warhead at the ship. The outer hull sparkles with intense heat. They still do nothing.

I fire another nuclear warhead. It hits their portside. Once again their hull sparkles in its radiant beauty.

I hear the voice of my daughter. Is this the only course of action that humans know? Why must wanton destruction be the only way that we treat encounters with the unknown? How long do these wars, if that is what they are, have to go on?

I hear the commanding officer screaming orders at me to destroy the ship. Yet I wonder if that is the right thing to do. Will the destruction of this ship really mean a better life for Una? Or a more sheltered one?

I see the ship begin to break up from our attack. I notice an escape pod come away from the ship. It is too small to be picked up by the sensors back on earth.

I let it go. The mothership explodes in a brilliant flash of light.

I attempt to slam my fist against the control panel but my hand goes through it. It seems to have no substance. What is going on here?

Your voyage is complete.

What? Whose voyage?

Your voyage to Kortana.

What?

Please remove you headset.

I remove the thing about my head and look around. This is not the ship I boarded back on earth. I can see the purple surface of a planet on the view screen.

Computer, where am I?

Kortana.

Is that my home world?

Yes.

I am not an earthman?

No.

Why did you let me believe that I was?

You must know that the earthman did spare your life when this escape pod left the ship. I know circumstances are not right at this moment for negotiations between our two worlds, but perhaps someday they will learn to be more tolerant of other races.

Yes, I remember now. Perhaps you are right. You may begin landing procedures. Only now can I understand the fear of the unknown that earth people have. Poor things."

And he sat there and cried. The smoky lights in that bar served as the shroud for this poor creature who had come to feel such despair and yet admiration for a race as proud yet impetuous as the human race.

As Rick and I left, I turned back and noticed that a tear of blue, white, and red left his right eye.

NACHO

The dust rose over the entryway into the El Cenizo Drive Inn as the truck pulled out, covering the *cenizos* on either side with its fine powder. The marquis read *"Santos vs. Las Momias de Guanajuato"*, a film that Role vividly remembered, but whose sound he never heard, since at this point in time, they lived close enough to the drive inn to see the images on the big screen, but whose sound could only be heard if it happened to be picked up by the wind and carried to them.

At a much later point in time, this would be a major intersection in Eagle Pass, but for now, it was simply another unevenly paved dusty road in the small southwest Texas town. As usual, the sweltering heat reminded him of how Dante had described the various levels of the inferno into which he descended. They passed the John Deer dealership, which would burn down so many years later, on the right side. From this vantage point, the entirety of the downtown area could be seen, even as the pollution from Piedras Negras, *en el otro lado*, covered the horizon with a grey and misty haze.

"When does the computer say that we're supposed to keep the accident from happening?", asked Rick not taking his eyes from the street ahead.

"According to this, the accident will take place at exactly 2:43 p.m.", as he examined his hand-held computer monitor.

"Does it say who this guy is? I don't even remember ever having met him. Or even heard of him for that matter."

"His name is Ignacio Chavez. He is a mechanic for the gasoline station on the corner of Main and Monroe."

"Says here that a gas leak will be ignited by a spark which will lead to an explosion which will level the building and cause structural damage to the library across the street and to the VFW building next door."

"What time is it now?" asked Rick, as he drove the truck down the hill to the downtown area.

"2:00 p.m. That means that we have to get there now. Find a parking space as soon as we get downtown.", said Role as he put away the computer.

After finding a place to park in front of the library, the two brothers walked across the street and into the working area of the garage. A man clad in grey, oil-stained coveralls approached them.

"Buenas tardes. ¿Les puedo ayudar en algo?", he asked.

"Buenas tardes. We're looking for Ignacio Chavez. Does he work here?" asked Role, as he looked around.

"Yo soy Ignacio Chavez. ¿Y ustedes quien son?"

"Mi nombre es Ricardo Diaz, y este es mi hermano, Rolando Diaz. We are here to help.", answered Rick.

"Look, I am a Catholic. I do not want to hear about another religion, y'know? My father was a Catholic. His grandfather was a Catholic."

"You don't understand. We are not here to talk about religion. What we need you to do is to get ahold of the gas company. Tell them that you need to report a gas leak."

"What gas leak? I don't smell a gas leak."

"Look, the leak is there. If you don't report it, it will cause an explosion that will level this building. Please, for your sake. Give them a call.", asked Role, trying to convince the man without giving away too much information.

"You guys must be crazy. But, I don't want to take no chances", said Ignacio as he walked into the business office and placed the call.

"I can't figure this one out", said Rick. "Every time we have gone on one of these trips, we have had to save ourselves from certain things that had to take place in very specific sequences. How does Mr. Chavez fit in?"

"I don't know. I've looked under personal references, and his name just doesn't come up."

Ignacio came back.

"They said they will send someone right over. They will shut down the gas, just to be sure. I just have one question: How do you know there is a gas leak?" he asked.

"We were walking by and our instruments detected it." answered Role.

"Are you with the gas company?"

"No, not exactly." answered Rick.

At this, they proceeded outdoors. Role put a dime into the soda machine a pulled out a soda bottle. He popped it open and handed it to Rick. Role then put another dime in and took out a second soda. After popping the cap off, he took a long hard drink. The cold liquid felt good as it went down his throat. The sweltering heat was growing evermore oppressive as the time approached 3:00 p.m. A car came up for a fill-up. Ignacio went up to serve the customer.

After about ten minutes, the gas man pulled up in his red truck. He went around the building checking all of the gas mains. He then proceeded inside to call his office. He shook his head as he came out.

"We sure got lucky on this one. There was a gas leak in the main gauge which leads to this building. Fortunately, we caught it in time. Mr. Chavez there probably saved some people's lives."

"He probably did." said Role, "He probably did."

SNAPSHOTS

A Moment in the Desert

The limbs of the mesquite swayed gently in the breeze as the lizard made its way up the side, grasping at the crevices of the bark, climbing slowly in the southwest Texas desert heat, as the mesquite pods waved in the all-too-scarce wind. In the distance two weary travelers appeared, first as hard-to-see stick figures, then as discernible beings.

Futuro

The future is one where everything that now exists will come together to create what can only be called the great American ideal. As history has shown us, Western civilization has grown because of its constant absorption and modification of elements from other cultures. So it will continue in the future. Physically, we will embody the very essence of this country--*e pluribus unum*--many being one. As such, we will be not one race, but many. Part Hispanic, Black, Asian, and Native

American. Culturally, we will come to celebrate the essence of every culture through our music, literature, art, and food. The elements of what we now are will form the great conglomeration of an ideal that will encompass every culture that is today a vital part of the American societal fabric.

Snow

The snow fell gently as the car slid to a slow halt. The temperature outside continued to fall way below the freezing level. The powdery snow resembled ghostly apparitions over the black asphalt roads as they danced and twisted at the passing of every car. Overhead, the sky loomed grey and dark, with no hope of having the sun peek through with its warm illuminating rays.

Roger Blackburn was a man in his early thirties who had spent most of his life living it backwards, only appreciating things in hindsight. When not engaged in that fruitful activity, he spent it dreaming of how things would one day be, if he ever won a million dollars, when he finally published his writings, when he sold the movie rights to his short stories. Reality, fate, or whoever controls our destiny, would perpetually see to it that none of these things would ever come to pass.

"Oklahoma doesn't usually get it this bad." he said. "The weather lady was sure it would blow over." Over the hill to his right he could see the lights from the long line of oncoming cars, moving at a snail's pace toward him.

¡HASTE EL BEHAVE O TE ESPANQUEO!: MUSINGS AND PREGUNTAS ON THE HISPANIC EXPERIENCE

ENTRE DOS CULTURAS

We live in an interesting time in the United States and in the world. Everything seems to be coming together and creating something entirely different. Very much like the original source, retaining qualities of the same, yet different. This text is an exploration of the creation of something wonderful in two countries and in two cultures. *Yo soy Mexicano*, but I am also American. Always on the fence, sitting between two ideals, two value systems, and two ways of doing things.

I tell people that when I approach any new task, I carry with me two tool boxes – the Mexican, and the American. I take a little from this one and a little from that one. What results is a unique perspective on life. *Soy dos culturas*, but I am one person.

If words like lariat, taco, and enchilada can make it into the English vocabulary, then why not words like encabronate, asustate, and apaciwaite?

By the same token, (no pun intended) if words like *troca, carro*, and *parqueadero* can make it into the Spanish vocabulary, then why can't words like *ansorris, pistafeado,* and *charapear* make it as well? On the border, we tend to blend two cultures, so why not two languages?

I have often wondered about the things that I have managed to put down in this document. These are indeed questions that have kept me awake at nights, even as I try to get under the *cobijas* and into a restful slumber.

Questions, comments, complaints, jokes, and gossip. *Preguntas, comentarios, quejas, chistes, y chismes.* Whatever it takes, as long as I am able to get some sleep, . . . eventually.

¿POR WHY?

Los Fishermen

Pues, que te cuento. The story goes *que estaban* two fisherman *pescando y ya era la hora* del lunch. But they had two buckets *de camarones* and they didn't want to lose them if they got out when they were away.

Y le dice un fisherman al otro, "Tenemos que cover them up. *Porque si no, se nos escapan.*"

"*Nombre,*" says the other fisherman, "*Nomas hasle* cover up *a esos, porque* they are American crabs."

"*¿Y esos?*"

"*Estos son* Mexican crabs. The minute one tries to climb out, the others will pull him *pa 'tras!*"

"*Hijole, que gacho! Pero he vato,* check that one out right there. He seems to be making it!"

"He's even shaking his tail at the rest of them."

"*Y tambien los esta* pinching."

"You know why? Because he is not a *camaron*. He is an *escorpion!*"

321

La familia

La familia es one thing *que es muy importante para nosotros los* Hispanics, *pero* it is one thing that can sometimes hold us back. I have heard too many kids in El Paso say that they would leave to go see other things that are beyond the Franklin Mountains, *pero* they can't because there don't want to leave behind their *familia*. They need to stay and take care of their brothers, sisters, uncles, aunts, *abuelos*, and their parents, *tambien*.

Lo que debería ser something that drives them to see what is out there beyond the city limits is what keeps them stuck *en la casa*. How can we fix *esta honda*? Well, we need to tell them *que* there are new experiences to be here out there *en el otro mundo*. They need to go out and live *sus vidas, porque nomas una tenemos*.

La familia is important, but they need to understand *que* they will be able to provide for them better if they take advantage *de la oportunidades que se les presentan*.

Religion

We as *Mexico-Americanos* tend to put a lot of faith in God. In fact, we don't do anything *si El no quiere*. What does this mean? Well, remember the last time you made plans or a date to meet someone? What did you say? *"Si Dios quiere."* "I will be there *si Dios quiere*. I will graduate the first in my family *si Dios quiere*." *Pero,* what happens *si Dios no quiere*? I guess you're in trouble.

Relationships

Many people say that *la cultura Mexicana* is very patriarchal, *que los hombres mandan. Pero,* did you ever stop to wonder *que si los hombres mandan,* why are there so many *corridos* where the man is crying for his lost love with a woman? I mean, did you ever see Vicente Fernandez cry for his woman? *Hijole,* that is power.

El Supernatural

When I was a kid and we went to the family reunions at Christmas in Allende, all the kids would sleep in the living room next to the kitchen in my Uncle Pedro's house. My uncles and aunts would gather around the kitchen table and tell ghost stories.

I still remember my mother telling the story of when she and my dad were just married and they stayed in my grandmother's house, which everyone knew was haunted. They had to sleep on the floor, and my mother *dice* to this day *que* she felt something grab her hand in the middle of the night. *Que* it was cold and soft, like *algodón.* To this day, I do not sleep with my hands hanging over the side of the bed, *porque nunca sabes,* you know?

Los TV Shows

Nosotros somos the oldest immigrants and yet we are the newest *inmigrantes también.* We were here *con Cristobal Colon* (Christopher Columbus in English), but we also just arrived yesterday. People seem to forget that we have a long history in this country. That we have been there when the greatest moments and turning points have taken place. *Pero*, does Hollywood notice this? Do they know that we are now the largest minority? Over 44 million, according to the US Census. We also have a spending power of over 950 billion dollars. Think they'll notice us soon? I bet they will.

Jaime Tiburcio Cuevas in Outer Space

Back in the sixties, there was a TV show *donde salía un bato, pero* I can't remember his name. I think it was *Jaime Tiburcio Cuevas. Y él era un* Captain *de un* starship. *Bien de aquellas*. It could go *con madre* into outer space. *Y toda la gente* couldn't even feel it. Not like when we were kids and had to ride in the back of the truck on the way to the groceries. *Con todo el pinche* wind in our hair. *Y llegábamos todos* uncombed *y* sweaty.

Pero, anyway, este Captain Cuevas used to hang out *con un bato que le decían Orejitas. Porque el bato siempre parecía que andaba* pissed. *Híjole, siempre con las* eyebrows *de lado y las* pointed *orejas*. Pues, Captain Cuevas y Orejitas tenían otro best friend *que era un doctor, pero ha de ver sido muy flaco, porque le decían el Huesitos.*

LOS NICKNAMES

Los Nicknames

When you are a *chavalio en el barrio*, you have to be very careful about the nicknames you get, *porque si no, se te queda*. Why is it that when we are *chavalios* we are deathly afraid of any nickname? Let me mention just a few of my cousins: *La Chana, La Goya, La Lila, el Pilín, el Pito, el Juanío, el Germancio, el Cora, La Pati, La Pochi, La Panca,* and *el Ponchin*.

In my own experience, I could have been *Tito, Nonano, Choche, Choche Maya,* and *el Prieto*, but fortunately, I ended up with *el Role*. My brother, Ricardo, ended up with *el Calín*.

My *primos* did not do as well as you can tell from the following:

- *El Pito* – his real name was Reynaldo, but when he was a kid, he could not pronounce it and instead *el Pito*, and it stuck.
- *La Lila* – *el Pito's* sister, whose real name was Lydia.

- *La Goya* – *el Pito's* other sister, whose real name I can't remember. *La Goya* stood for *gorda*. I guess she was a little heavy as a child.

- *La Chaín* – short for Rosario, *el Pito's* youngest sister

- *El Meme* – Manuel, I think.

- *El Pilín* – short for Alfredo, and you know the rest.

- *El Juanío* – this one is a little obvious.

- *La Pochi* – Her real name was *Flor*. Go figure.

- *La Panca* – I honestly don't know what her real name is.

- *El Ponchín* – Short for Alfonso.

- *El Germansío* – Pronounced with an "h" and short for German.

- *El Cora* – Loved quarters, the coins, as a kid.

- *La Chana* – Sandra, *el Cora's* sister.

- *El Grío* – Short for *Oscarío*

- *El Riche* – Short for Ricardo; variations include: *El Chicho, el Rica, el Rico*

- *El Guile* – Short for Guillermo; variations include: *el Willie*

- *El Nacho* – Short for Ignacio

- *El Conejo* – Because he had two buck teeth in the ninth grade.

- *El Chutaso* – Because he was always doing things in a bad way.

- *El Logle* – Because they couldn't say ugly.
- *El Calavera* – He looked like a *calavera*.
- *El Ganzo* – Ninety-nine pounds and had a long neck.
- *El Gato* – Because he always fought like a cat.

You would not want the word *pinche* between el/la and your nickname, because that meant you in some kind of trouble, or that they didn't like you much (i.e. *el pinche* Riche, etc.).

Of course, there were other ways to claim connection to your *familia*. You were usually identified by your nickname as it related to your parents.

- *German el de Maye*
- *Martin el de Estela*
- *Role el de Olga*
- *Nelli la de Rosa*
- *Sandra la de Oscar*
- *Chuy el de Tina*

At other times, nicknames took on a life all their own. Many times they were completely unrelated to the name or were something that sounded like it.

- *La Lechusa* – Jesus
- *La Mosca* – Oscar
- *El Asco* – Oscar

- *El Speedy* – Espiririon
- *La Espi* – Esperanza
- *El Chuletas*
- *El Piojo*
- *La Chela*
- *El ehporque* – The teacher swatted him on the behind once and he didn't know why.
- *El Chalío*
- *El Chencho*
- *La Chencha*
- *Beto el Cuchillo*

Bueno, pues, just take care what you call someone because it may be with them the rest of their life. *Nunca sabes*.

El Animalón
Many times white kids don't do too well *en la frontera*, especially in elementary school. There was this *chavalía* when I was in Graves Elementary whose name was Annie Malone. It didn't help that she was chubby and that the rest of the kids didn't like her too much. When she was introduced, most of the class heard *animalón*, much to the misfortune of poor Annie.

UNOS THOUGHTS CHISTOSOS

Café Moco
El otro dia I had a café moco.
Don't you mean a café moca?
No, I had a café *moco*. I accidentally sneezed in my coffee!

El Soothsayer
When I was a *chavalio*, there was this *vato que segun él*, he could tell the future. He said that the Mexican *peso iba ser* worth more *que el* American dollar. *Tambien dijo que* Al Gore *iba ser el President de los* United States. *Este vato*, he always said one thing, *pero salia otra cosa*, so we didn't call him Nostradamas. We called him *Nuestro* Dumbass.

Estado Grande Perro Chiquito
Chihuahua. Is the state named after the dog or is

the dog named after the state? The largest state in Mexico named after a puny pooch. Only the locals know for sure.

"¡Haste el behave o te espanqueo!"

There was this one time when I was young and was doing laundry at a laundromat. There was a young woman there with three kids that were running wild all over the place. Finally, when she was at the end of her rope, she screamed at the top of her lungs, *"¡Háganse el behave o los espanqueo!"*

WHAT WE SAY AND HOW WE SAY IT

What We Say and How We Say It

There are words that are alike or the same in English and Spanish. The listing below contains a few words that can almost be used interchangeably in both languages.

Agony	Agonía
Alleviate	Aliviar
Castigate	Castigar
Chocolate	Chocolate
Cicatricize	Cicatrizar
Curiosity	Curiosidad
Dedicate	Dedicar
Delicious	Delicioso
Diabolic	Diabólico
Facile	Fácil
Inculcate	Inculcar

331

Infamy	Infamia
Justice	Justicia
Lament	Lamentar
Maize	Maíz
Matriculate	Matricular
Masticate	Masticar
Navigate	Navegar
Optimist	Optimista
Penultimate	Penúltima
Particular	Particular
Singular	Singular
Triumph	Triunfo
Violate	Violar

A Quick Reference List Of Words
That should be in a Spanglish Dictionary but aren't

English

Almuersate: to take part of breakfast. (i.e. Since it was early morning, I *almuersated* a couple of eggs and toast.)

Apestate: to wreak or to smell really bad (i.e. The limburger cheese really *apestated* so I had to put it in a plastic bag.)

Apaciwaite: to behave or to settle down (i.e. The kids were being rowdy so I told them to *apaciwaite* themselves.)

Asustate: to freighten or scare (i.e. She was very *asustated* after she saw the scary movie and could not sleep all night.)

Ayudate: to help (i.e. She needed help, so I *ayudated* her with the groceries.)

Chingate: to irritate, bother, or otherwise mess with (i.e. He was *chinganding* so much that I told him to just leave me alone.)

Cocinate: to cook; the act of preparing a meal (i.e. I *cocinated* for about four hours before I finished getting dinner ready.)

Encabronate: to irritate or anger; to make irritable or angry (i.e. Since he did not get things his way, he became very *encabronated.*)

Enchilate: to suffer the after effects of having eaten a very hot pepper or spice (i.e. The jalapeño was very hot, so I was very *enchilated.*)

Esperate: to wait (i.e. I told him to *esperate* for me while I took care of a few things.)

Fregate: to bother or irritate (i.e. I told him not to be *freganding* so much because I had work to do.)

Gargant: throat (i.e. After coughing so much, my *gargant* was very soar.)

Grenia: hair (i.e. My *grenia* is way too long, so I need to get it cut.)

Ladrate: to bark (i.e. The dog was *ladrating* too much, so I had to bring him inside.)

Limpiate: to clean or straighten up (i.e. The house was a mess so I *limpiated* it before the guests arrived.)

Machucate: to crush or bruise (i.e. I didn't get my hand out in time and the door *machucated* my finger.)

Manihate: to steer an automobile. (i.e.: I was *manihating* way too fast when I got a ticket.) see: draivear

Olvidate: to forget (i.e. I get so busy sometimes that I even *olvidate* my own name.)

Osic: mouth or snout (i.e. He didn't like it when I told him to shut his *osic* and be quiet.)

Pasiate: to ride or carry (i.e. We missed our exit, so we *pasiated* in our car for about an hour before we got back to it.)

Pat: foot (i.e. My *pats* were very tired after I walked so much.)

Peyiscate: to pinch (i.e. I was falling asleep so she *peyiscated* me to stay awake.)

Pick: to prick or sting (i.e. I *picked* my finger with the safety pin. The bee picked me in the arm.)

Quem: to burn (i.e. I *quemmed* my hand when I touched the hot iron.)

Regate: to irrigate; to ruin or spoil something. (i.e. He really *regated* it when he told everyone what I had told him.)

Spanish

Ansorris: disculpas (ejemplo– ¡Aquí no me vengas con tus *ansorris*!)

Beiquear: el acto de cocer algo en el orno (ejemplo – Te *beiquié* un pastel para el día de tu santo.)

Cachear: el acto de ferear un cheque a dinero en efectivo. (ejemplo – Voy a ir a *cachear* el cheque antes del fin de semana.)

Charapear: el hacer quieto o silencio (ejemplo – ¡No hagan ruido! ¡Ya *charapense*!)

Cofear: El acto de tocer (ejemplo: Estaba *cofeando* mucho y la tuve que llevar con el doctor.)

Draivear – el mantener el control de un coche. (Ejemplo: Venia *draiveando* muy rápido cuando le dieron un tiquete.) ref: manihate

Estinquear – el dar el mal olor. (Ejemplo: El Chuletas *estinqueava* mucho porque no usaba desodorante.)

Imeilear: el acto de mandar un correo electronico (ejemplo – Le *imeilié* las direcciones para que no se le olvidaran.)

Pistafear: el estar enojado o irritado (ejemplo – Después de que averiguamos, se fue bien *pistafiado*.)

Teiquerear: el tomar cuidado de si mismo (ejemplo – *Teiquereate* si vas a tener buena salud.)

Afterword

There is an old Mexican saying, *"Ingles no aprendiendo y español olvidando."* I am not learning English and I am forgetting my Spanish. It would seem that as we continue to merge our two cultures, we are doing this more and more. What seems to be happening is that both languages are having a direct influence on the development of the other. If this continues to happen in the near future, who knows what our two languages will sound like in fifty years.

BIOGRAPHY

Biography of Rolando Josué Diaz

Rolando Josué Diaz was born in Allende, Coahuila, Mexico. At the age of a few months, his parents, brought him, along with his older brother, Rick, to Eagle Pass, Texas. Growing up, physically, culturally, and linguistically between two worlds, Rolando developed an appreciation for and an understanding of the nuances of both the Mexican and the American societies. He holds a B.A. in Drama from The University of Texas at Austin, and M.A. in Drama from the University of North Texas, an M.A. in English from Texas Woman's University, an M.A. in Bilingual Education / ESL from The University of Texas of the Permian Basin and has earned post-graduate hours at the University of Kansas and at The University of Texas at El Paso. His career in higher education in universities in the midwest and west Texas spans over two decades. He currently lives in Odessa, Texas with his wife, Lewanda, and their three Chihuahuas.

CPSIA information can be obtained
at www.ICGtesting.com
Printed in the USA
LVHW051619180322
713802LV00008B/315

9 781432 704933